<u>The Suspense</u>

By:

Bryan "Nappy" Vereen

aKA

Top!ck

AkA

The Legendary King Author The Booking Book King

From: Put it down for my town that's WILD CITY, KANZISS!!!

To:

Anyone that has dreams, had dreams, sleeps in any kind of way and those that have or have not lived a dream.....

<u>Blurb</u>

Isn't it frazy how the same one mind could have hundreds to even over a thousand or so dreams alone in one year? All different, all creative, all with some kind of message or meaning? WE literally could have hundreds of dreams a year and maybe some of US reaching 1,000 or so a year. So many mental movies, scripts, drama, love, scary, images, suspense, what the fucks, and ideas given and made by US when OUR body is at rest and WE aren't even thinking hard, in the most relaxed state of mind. What does that right there tell YOU? How do OUR dreams come to US? Where do OUR dreams go? Where do YOUR dreams go? What do YOU do with them? How do YOU act on them? Let's go inside of OUR mind and see with OUR eyes closed and what WE see and think about when WE are literally doing nothing but sleeping and getting well needed rest. What are WE being told? What are WE being shown? The PROcess of night, write, type, and recite these dreams into reality and seeing what I've seen with MY eyes closed and to show and explain it to the world. Also, the suspense of never finishing a dream and what WE are going to do to acknowledge it and how YOU would finish YOUR dream and how others would as well with the power of the mind. Here WE go! Asiago!!!!!!

THESE DREAMS ARE CLEARLY FROM MY SUBCONSCIOUS MIND WHILE THE BODY IS RESTING, BUT THE MIND IS CONSTANTLY WORKING. FROM THE SUBCONSCIOUS MIND TO THE CONSCIOUS MIND WRITING THEM DOWN. GET READY TO LEARN WHAT PROGRAMS, PERCEPTION, AND THOUGHT TEACHES AND INGRAINS INTO THE DEEP MIND AND MENTALITY. EVERYTHING inFLUences and YOUR DREAMS AND THINKING IS A GREAT EXAMPLE OF THIS..............

<u>The Fast Foreward:</u>

The more-I-wrote ,the more-I-spoke/ Took-notes made good-quotes before-I-woke/

*I write MY dreams as I realitize MY life! This book goes to all of those that have dreams and need an idea of what to do with them. For the people, places, and things I have seen in MY life and in MY dreams that are INside of MY mind and body that touch MY soul. It's **<u>YOUnique</u>** to say and notice something like that. WE all have dreams or have had a dream and it's up to US to do something with them. I want to thank EVERYONE and EVERYTHING that has been a part of MY life whether on a good term or a bad term because someway or somehow YOU have INspired thought and visions that I dream about and MY outlook of life. Who knows? More than likely with the people that read this book I could INspire visions, thoughts, and dreams for something for Y'ALL to realitize and act on as well! I give thanks to The Higher Power, MY EXperiences, MY past, MY present present of presence, MY future, the people I have had in MY lifetime, the good and the bad of ANYONE and EVERYTHING! I want to give thanks to MYSELF for having the motivation and determination to act out on MY thoughts. Also, I want to thank YOU for taking the time for opening this book and somewhat judging a book for it's cover, but getting to understand what's INside of this book and MY mind and YOUR mind as well! Asiago!!!*

Slanguage/Flowcabulary:

Dizzamn= *Damn/ A "DDDDAAAAAAAAMMMMMMMMMNNNNNNNNNN" moment*

Dub Dub= *A White Woman*

Feezies= *Females/Women/Girls*

Fool(s)= *Friend Or A person*

Frazy= *Fuckin' Crazy*

Fuhh= *Fuck*

Fuhdd/Fuhhd= *Fucked*

Mawfuckaz= *Motherfuckers*

Momster In Law= *A mother in law that is difficult to be around, negative, & shugly*

Realitize= *To make dreams reality. To make YOUR life a living dream. To make trueness.*

Shexy= *Sexy/Seductive/Good Looking*

Shugly= *Shit Ulgy/ Ugly As Fuhh/ Ugly As Fuck*

Smash= *Have sex with, fuck, INtimate*

Trueness= *True/ Being True/Factual*

YOUnique= *A unique YOU. EVERYTHING in YOU that makes YOU amazing and great.*

ARE Y'ALL PREPARED FOR WHAT GOES ON IN THE SUBCONSCIOUS THOUGHTS OF A GENIUS WHEN HIS BODY IS AT REST, BUT THE MIND IS IN IDLE MODE????????????

ASIAGO!!!!!!!!!!

The Colombian Feezy Timptation Likes--- _So I'm at work on my screen print press that is next to this skinny Colombian girl's press. She's been here for about about 6 or so months now and she's always given me these weird looks. I don't know if these looks are "Ugh! Stay the fuck away from me!" Or if they're the "I think you're cute and I want you to notice me checking you out." kind of look. She looks good, but I'm not worried about her like that. I mean if she wants me to **smash** I'mma **smash** that's if she presents it to me other than that I'm not going out of my way to get at her like that. Now my fool Timptation has been working here as well and he's alway press supporting on her machine as an excuse to always talk and be around her. This fool is a trip! Anyways as I'm walking around my press I look up and see him and her both looking at me then they both just smile and laugh. I look at them and say "Whatever." As they looked at me and laughed again. I already know that Timptation is definitely trying to be funny and this is his way of even talking to her or even being this close to her. This fool Timptation has almost gotten me to believe that he has a crush on me too. This fool is something else. How as a man can you be trying to get close to a **feezy** that is paying attention to and flirting with me as you're trying to flirt with her? This fool is retarded. So I get back to focusing on my press and that's when……………………………_

Garden Of The Broads--- _So I'm in the beautiful Colorado state and beautiful Colorado Springs. Why? Because I'm from Kansas and Colorado has some of the most beautiful mountains and scenery I've experienced and it's literally right next to my home state of Kansas. I'm riding around in this huge ass tall white truck with the darkest tint on windows, huge tires, and stilts on the truck that stands about 10 or so feet high. As I'm cruising through The Garden Of The Broads I'm seeing some beautiful ass rocks, mountains, paths, and women! The weather is nice and so are the women out here. I might not go back to Kansas because everytime I come to Colorado it just keeps getting nicer and nicer with more and more reasons for staying out here even longer. Women of all colors, races, and nationalities that's going to get me thinking irrationalities! I'm driving by slowly as women are posing and propped up on these rocks, the roads, and sidewalks. Everything around here is already beautiful enough so to have these women all around makes this place even more flawlessly beautiful or some other words that are close to describing what I'm seeing, but still not quite there. After riding through and scoping this place out as the sun is slowly going down that's when I'm not sure if my eyes were playing tricks on me, but I swear I could have seen some of these women turn into nocturnal animals, ghosts, wolves, coyotes, possums, goats, bobcats, etc. from the corner of my eye as my truck rolls past them, but when I would look back the women that I had just drove_ *past were gone. I got to second guessing myself and thinking I'm just seeing things because it's late out and because before that I was in the heat for most of the day and because I'm hungry as __fuhh__. I decide to just drive through here tomorrow when I have more sunlight. As I'm driving past the rest of these outdoor women and feeling the temperature drop outside I got to thinking about how and why they have curfews out here and if certain people have ended up missing here due to trying to get and find these women after hours. What happens to those people and bodies? I don't know, but it definitely had me second guessing these women as well and what truly happens to them and what their intentions are. How do they protect themselves? I'm just so zoned out into figuring out if everything is as it's viewed as visually, but not in reality. Then that's when "screech!!!"......I slammed on my brakes hard as fuhh as I had almost drove my truck off of an unfinished road or bridge that just automatically cuts off and is a cliff 80 or so feet above what's below it. "What the FUCK?!" I said out loud as my heart started thumping so loud and hard. I instantly built up a sweat. "What the fuck?! Why wouldn't they put up a sign or put up flashing lights or something especially in a zone with so many distractions and attractions around it?" I look over the hood of my truck as I'm already 10 feet above everything so that would have been a 90 or so foot drop from where I'm at. I see so much of the city and it's bright lights and traffic and it's beautiful. I put my truck in reverse to just go the opposite way or whatever before they close the park down and I have to sleep here overnight or run my truck through the gate. __Frazy__ thing about me going in reverse is the fact that those women are appearing back up and everything in my back window is the sunny day time again, but when I look forwards while in reverse it's night time. I look over my shoulder and behind me again and it's bright day time with women behind and I look forwards again while in reverse and it's night time. I'm looking like "What the fuck?!" Until I ended up running something over so I look behind me and it's bright and sunny as I'm leaving some nice Colorado Springs neighborhood and…………………………………....*

__Stank Breath In Business---__ *I'm in this doctors office walking away from the receptionist window to this available seat next to this White family. As I have my beanie on and my tank top with my muscles popping out everywhere. I see this little White boy from that White family just stare at me as I walk closer and closer towards them and I sit down right next to him in the open chair. Now instead of doing what most people do when they're out in public and sitting next to strangers and being either on their phone or watching the TV, I sat down next to that little White boy and I pulled my wallet out to get my pen and paper and I start to write some rhymes down to pass the time and this kid is looking over at me and he asks me "How can you write so small and read it so small too?" That's when I looked over at him and I said "That's so no one else can read it." Sarcastically and that's when he cocked his head back far and said "Wow dude!" As I smiled and laughed at him and that's when he said "Your breath smells like total SHIT!" That's when everyone looked over at us and began laughing and that's when I…………………*

__A Dub With An L---__ *So this feezy I know named "A-Dub" is on trial for the final court hearing and sentencing for a serious assualt of this other feezy that was fucking her man or vice versa, her man was fucking because he's known to fuck anyone and anything that A-Dub brings around. The talks at the beginning of this brutal assault case were about 30 years in prison* *especially with her priors and being to prison before and multiple other fights. With all the time she could be facing and with all of the time to think about her life and how it has gotten to this point and not even 30 years old A-Dub has been thinking a lot about changing her life and the people she's been around and attracted to, but she's also scared that it may be too late to change now with the possibilities of being around life changing people that could have life plus more in a facility where mistakes, excuses, wrongfully accused, dangerous, hurt, pained, and outcasts out of societies individuals are put. As the trial is set and everyone is told to rise as the judge steps into the courtroom, that's when…………………………..*

Prank City Bus--- *So my maintain and I are getting onto this bus that can only be rode on whenever you plan to pull a prank on someone. The frazy and funny thing about this bus though is that only hardcore and avid YouTube watchers know about this bus and other people do, but you have to be a dedicated viewer, commenter, and subscriber to even set up a date and a prank on the video. The way this bus works though is that it almost looks exactly like any other city bus across major cities in the United States, but the differences could be the cameras and the energy in these buses unless you have some really good actors and actresses. You have to schedule a date and make the payment in advance, but everything else is like calling an Uber or a Lyft and waiting for them to pull up. The Prank City Buses can record multiple pranks at one time and they allow you to have your prank video as well, but obviously since they are the bigger platform they will get the most views and interactions. My maintain has no idea at all about this Prank City Bus as she's not much of a YouTube watcher or into watching pranks in such like that so this is going to be funny as fuhh as I can't wait to see her face. We step onto the bus and as soon as my maintain walks past the bus driver I look at the bus driver and I start smiling big as she smiles at me knowing about the prank that I have planned. The more and more steps through the walkway to find a seat my heart started thumping heavily and my anticipation was going up. My maintain is still ahead of me and I'm looking around and not trying to make it look too obvious that I'm looking for cameras. As I'm looking around that's when I heard my maintain scream so I jumped and I hurried up and turned my head her direction and she had flowers, red roses in her hand and that's when the bus takes off while I'm still in the aisle and I jerk back and I fall on my ass as everyone is looking and laughing at me. My maintain turns around and looks down at me as she has her hand on the pole and one hand on her roses and she says "Are you okay?" That's when I slowly stood up almost in disbelief that she didn't fall because I've been on way more city buses than she has, but I guess since she hasn't she's being way more cautious and had a pole in her hand. I say to her "Yuh. I'm good. I wasn't expecting all of that though." Then that's when my maintain puts the flowers up to her nose then up to mines and she tells me to smell the flowers and then she tells me about how some fool by the name of Bryant Guller got her the roses. I'm thinking in my head "I thought you didn't like flowers. What the fuck?!" But I guess I said that out loudly "I thought you didn't like flowers. What the fuck?! Plus who the fuck is Bryant Guller and why is another fool giving you flowers and why are you accepting them?" That's when the whole bus says "Uh oh!" Then that's when my maintain says "He got them for me for my birthday and at least he fucking remembered to get me something!" Then that's when the whole bus had said "Damn!" And then that's when the bus driver had slammed onto the brakes so hard that I lost my footing and I flew backwards and the last thing I remembered was seeing everyone hanging on tight to poles or their seats and myself flying backwards and then………………………*

Her Mom In The Shower--- *So uh, here I am. I'm at the in-laws house in what use to be my maintain and I's bathroom except for the fact that my mother in law is getting undressed right in front of me as I'm in a drowsy not so sure if this is really happening mindset right now. She's undressing in front of me as if it's no big deal and I see her saggy titties drop about 5 inches lower than I thought they sat, but to me they're still titties so it still turns me on. Her skin is wrinkly and saggy, but she's naked so it still turns me on. As the heat from the shower steams up the whole bathroom that's when she opens up the shower curtain and steps in slowly making sure that I could see her pussy better while her legs are open with one foot barely touching the tub floor and the other foot on the bathroom floor. She gives me this look of "Come and get it!" Before she fully steps into the shower and closes the curtain that's when…………………..*

Writing Rhymes--- *I'm seated on this chair with my small sheet of paper and pen in my hands. I have a few words jotted down on my sheet that I heard and I liked that I plan on rhyming them and matching with other words. As I'm zoned in and locked onto these words that's when words started coming to my mind that rhyme and that's when………………………..*

That Home Insurance Meeting--- *Here I am inside of this business as I had an appointment to speak with these two guys about home insurance. You know, big boy responsible adult goals. This company is a well known company not just locally, but nationwide as well. What this company does is provide a lot of honest and open conversations all while livestreaming on their YouTube channel. Which, this is great coverage, delivers great answers, and you can literally see their success rate, but this also allows lots of people to know about both your personal business and your home business. Also, your finances could be talked about which the viewer with an intention of negativity and scamming could harvest a lot of information about everyone on the livestreams. As I entered the store I saw this older Black guy and this older White guy that smiled and greeted me into their business and to follow them towards the two chairs towards the end of the store where there is a tripod stand and smartphone on it. I followed them towards the chairs and the tripod stand as they seemed very friendly and I'm honestly surprised at how well they knew me. It must be because I'm a local sensation with my dumbbell walks and all. We all take a seat in our chairs. Those 2 businessmen in the chairs right beside one another and my single chair about 5 to 6 or so feet across from them. We are set up and all checking if we are comfortable or need any water etc. So far so good and about 10 seconds later as the older White guy titles the livestream and sits back down as the livestream is about to begin that's when we began. General questions about home insurance are being brought up, price ranges, packages, what to know and what to look for, rates, insurances, coverage, etc….after question after question was being answered and we were approaching an hour on the livestream that's when we began to wrap things up as we covered a lot of important things. That older White guy had stood up again to go towards the smartphone and tripod stand to end the livestream and to upload it. You want to know something frazy? For their age I'm happy to know and see how well they also utilize technology and social media for promotion on their business which has served them well. We all stand up from our chairs and thank one another as we walk back towards the front desk by the entrance door. The older Black guy asks me "So everything was answered for you and you are good on everything?" That's when I looked at the* *both of them and I asked "So none of the personal questions anyone asks, tells, or gets answered on your livestream doesn't scare y'all or the clients for some scammer that may be watching and listening?" That's when they both lightly laughed, but then they said "Great question. We have been asked that before. First off, we have a couple of people on a laptop with every livestream we do that will bleep out certain things while live or even blur out some things if needed to. Also, any and everyone who watches we can see. We can see IP addresses, locations, and accounts. We are good. You are good. Trust me we wouldn't be as successful and trusted as a company if we didn't already think about this and planned it out." That's when I looked at them and responded with "I needed to hear that. I just didn't want to assume." Then that's when those 2 guys said "You're good. Thank you!" As I shook both of their hands and walked out of the front doors and…………………………………*

<u>Broken Glass, Driving Fast? And Snoop Dogg's Smoke Party Last---</u> *So guess the fuck what?! Here I am so excited to come home and relax, but as soon as I unlock the door to my house I see a house full of **<u>mawfuckaz</u>** that my maintain is friends with and even one of my managers at my job named Dani. They're excited to see me and I'm excited to see them until I look around the house and in the kitchen I see broken glass on the fucking floor! "What the fuck?! Are y'all fucking serious?! Who did this and just fucking left it?!" I yelled as everyone's party smiles and dancing had gone away and the music had stopped. My fucking snow globes, well the rest of the snow globes that weren't broken are now broken as the kitchen floor is wet, has glitter, and big chunks and small chunks of glass all over the floor that nobody seemed to care to pick up. I don't know if it was one of these dumb ass drunk fools that did it or if my youngest son had broken the rest, but either way I'm mad as fuhh about it. These fools are looking at me as if I'm a piece of shit for ruining a party and destroying everybody's good vibes, but come on! These people are in my place getting drunk and dumb and not even caring or worried about my stuff being broken or about their safety either. I walk to the kitchen and I see this big ass piece of glass on the floor that could easily be seen. As bad as I wanted to stomp the fuhh out of that glass or just throw it behind me to hit someone in the crowd, I decided to just leave. I walked past everyone as they looked at me in disgust. I open my front door and I slam it behind me as I step outside. I'm mad as fuhh and I could hear some of them say shit about me as I left my house, but I knew that if I had gone back in there it would have been a fight or me getting jumped. The music is turned back on inside of my house. I get into the Community Car that my hometown of Manhattan, Kansas aka Wild City, Kanziss now provides which is a major step above the bus transportation, the Green Apple bikes, electric scooters, etc. Now to have a Community Car that's electric at that that allows people to basically be their own Uber or Lyft or taxi cab driver is unique and helpful to a lot of locals that don't have a car or need one temporarily. I swipe my drivers license at the door which unlocks the door after a quick scan to verify you are liable and able to drive. Once the door unlocks you are then to sit in your seat and to make the adjustments needed to make your ride as comfortable as can be. Then it's as if you are in a photo booth as your picture is taken just to verify that you are the one with your driver's license, then you are to blow within this one box to verify if you have been drinking or smoking. These cars go hard and are great and take many measures and precautions before you start your process of driving. You also need to have insurance for your vehicle and you are to digitally sign a waiver and scan your credit or debit card or to even use cash to pay for your* *time and mileage within these Community Cars. I am now ready to leave a place that just a few moments ago I was happy and excited to be at until I saw what I saw. Nobody gives a fuck as long as they have a place to party at. I'm pissed, but I have to get the fuhh away from those fools before I end up doing and saying some shit that's going to fuck up my place, my relationships, friendships, and my life. I hate driving when mad, but I can't get it out of my mind that fools and feezies would do that to me and not give a fuck. I'm leaving and coming up Tuttle Creek Boulevard just so zoned out and trying to get that shit out of my mind. I'm turning at the stop light turning left past this liquor store and passing Blue Hills as I'm going towards Flint Hills Place. I take a fast turn and I want to punch my steering wheel so bad, but that'll charge me extra. As I drive up the hill I see flashing lights behind me and I'm thinking "Fuck?! What the fuck?!" As I look down at my speed to see that I was speeding. I was 7 miles over. "Fuck!" I drive more to get up the hill so it's not at a slant and puts a strain on the brakes and the car. I go up the hill some more to turn left right beside Flint Hills Place. "You see! This is why I hate to drive mad, but this is my fault." I say out loud. Frazy thing about the car pulling me over I notice that it's not your regular cop car in my hometown and that it looks like a mall security car with the yellow flashing lights on the top of it. Out steps out these two Black feezies. They walk slowly to my car on both sides. One skinny which is on my side and one fat which is on the passenger's side. They tapped on the glass so I rolled both windows down and they both said at the same time "You do know that when you speed in these cars for over a 10 second period….." Then they stopped and looked at one another and that's when the fat Black feezy finished by saying "The car sends a signal to local authorities and with your card and driver's license scanned we already know who you are." I looked at both of them and I said "Dizzamn." Then that's when the skinny Black girl says "So, Mr. Vereen. Mr. Bodybuilder. Big buff muscles. You're coming with us!" I unbuckled my seat belt and stepped out of the car not even thinking about my card still being charged by the minute as I'm out. I'm told to follow these 2 feezies as they opened up their back doors and put me in the back. They then drove off as I'm looking at the Community Car and I asked them "What about my card being charged?" That's when they say "You're good sweetie. When we report an arrest or even when you're out of the car for 15 minutes or when you shut it off it cuts off payment time." That's when I say "Asiago! Cool, but why am I arrested? Usually it's just a quick ticket." That's when they say "Yuh, but since everyone knows who you are you're coming with us." As they drive up the rest of the hill passing Flint Hills Place and they turn into these 2 fat goofy party type White feezies. That's when they turn around and they say "It's party time! Mr. BodyBuilder you're coming to Snoop Dogg's Smoke Party with us! We don't see you out except for with your workouts and everyone's curious with how you party and lots of girls wanna fuck you!" That's when I say "That's funny. I don't drink though, but I guess I'll go to this party since the party at my house pissed me off." That's when those 2 dub dubs screamed and yelled "Aye!" In excitement. As we go down the Manhattan Avenue steep hill and I'm lightly laughing thinking about how it went from me leaving a party to being pulled over by Black feezies that turned into White feezies to now going to a Snoop Dogg Smoke Party somewhere on K-State campus…...Next thing you know I'm on K-State Campus somewhere inside of this huge building on the floor as rap music is being played. Snoop Dogg is on the floor talking to people and being cool. He's just checking everything out and interacting and not acting as if he's too good to talk to people. As I look around at the party I notice a fool that him and I have not gotten along with in years. This* fool White Nashty which is one of my ex's named C's husband. I walk up to this fool and he looks nervous, but it's time to squash shit. What I did with his wife was fuhhd up and I can be the bigger person to admit that. This fool has every right to not like me and even hate me, but I'm going to get this off of my chest while him and I are in the same place. He looks at me nervously and that's when I say "Aye my daw. I just want to apologize for my past selfishness and not being considerate of the results and reactions of my actions for the people it would affect in the long-run. I was the wrong-one that ruined relationships because my relationship with myself was self hurt and hatred. You don't have to accept my apology, but it does make me feel better about myself to admit to you in person that I'm sorry and I mean it." That's when he looked at me eye to eye and he looked as if he was about to cry. To be honest with you I almost cried seeing that he was about to cry. That's when we had literally walked away from one another in two opposite directions. He had walked off to my right and I had walked away to the left. As I continued walking that's when I had seen this young White fool in a business suit with a Snoop Dogg afro walk off onto the dance floor and I continued to walk that direction until those 2 Black feezies and those 2 White feezies had rushed up to me and they…………………………

The 50 Cent Hustle & Weirdness--- So I'm in my maintain and I's room on our bed with our youngest son. My maintain is in the front room sleeping on the couch with 3 blankets on her and one of those blankets is mine. She's not feeling good so she fell asleep early. While I'm on the bed and my son is coming down from all his jumping because he knows it's about to be bedtime soon that's when I pulled out one of the books that I've been anxious to read "Hustle Harder" by 50 Cent. I've been so excited to read this book since before I clicked it to go into my cart online. I look at the cover of the book as I read everything on the outside before flipping the cover open. I read the inside of the book and the shout outs and preface of the book as I'm getting closer and closer to reading this book, I'm getting so excited. After reading the shout outs and preface that's when I heard a weird noise or something out in the front room. I stood up from the bed and looked at my son to see that he was asleep. Then I slowly stepped out of the bedroom saying "Chicana. Chicana! Was that you?" Thinking it was my maintain that made that noise. She didn't say anything so I slowly stepped out of our room and to the kitchen. I could hear something lightly move somewhere in the trailer. The thing about our trailer is that there are so many creeks in the floor so it's so sensitive. I walk through the kitchen and to the front room to see my maintain sleeping on the couch still as she slowly turns and says something, but she's in such a deep sleep. That's when I was about to say her name, but then that's when I heard that same sound again from our hallway. "What the fuhh?!" I lightly said. As I was about to look down the hallway that's when a green bowl came rolling down the hallway. I flinched and my heart started thumping louder and harder. I have to see what it is though because I have to protect my family. I'm the only one awake so I have to defend myself the best I can. I slowly stepped to look down the hallway as the green bowl that rolled past me stopped rolling. As I'm looking down the dark hallway I still hear that weird noise. I look down and I see two glowing eyes low to the hallway floor. "What the fuhh is that?!" As I'm trying to focus in closer before I decide to get a weapon to defend myself from whatever this thing is. Then as I focus in that's when I see that it's my maintain and I's kitten we once had living with *us. "How the fuhh did it get back into our home though? What is it doing here?" Is what I asked myself totally confused and curious and that's when……………………………*

C. Deli In Town--- *So my daw C. Deli is in town and we haven't seen each other in years. To be honest, I believe the last time I honestly saw this fool was probably 2011 and that was only for about 3 minutes or so before my maintain and I at the time had to call the cops on one of my ex's for being by us at a gas station when we had a restraining order against her obsessive and frazy ass. Anyways, C. Deli and I are walking towards this parking lot as we are bringing up funny stories since the day we met as teenagers and what all has happened and changed for us over the years. This fool had gotten married and had kids since I had last seen him in person and I have had kids too, but no marriage yet. Then that's when I brought up our fool G-Mo to C. Deli and how we had all been friends since juvenile delinquents, literally. I brought up how G-Mo was working in Wild City, Kanziss for a little bit, but was bored and how his wife and him were having problems before he got transferred back out of state. The three of us have gone through some frazy things, but have all grown up and experienced more about life and adults than we did as teenagers. Then that's when I changed the topic to my maintain and I after the whole G-Mo and his wife story. I looked around the parking lot and I looked at C. Deli and I said "My maintain wants to go out with her friend Tuff tonight. Now usually I don't trip, but I've been losing lots of trust for her to be honest with you. Plus she wants to go out when I leave town too. I think it's frazy and weird and I have nothing against her friend Tuff, but Tuff is single and things between my maintain and I have not been the same." That's when my daw C. Deli gives me this look of "**Dizzamn**, well that switched up quickly!" And that's when…………………………………*

The Preparation--- *So it's all of us in my maintain's mom's car. It's my father in law driving, **momster in law** in the passenger seat, my maintain in the back seat behind her dad with our oldest son beside her, our youngest son beside me as we are seated behind my momster in law and I'm by the car door. We're passing Cico Park in my hometown of Wild City, Kanziss going up the hill and things have been hectic as we have been told to evacuate our homes as a mass riot and all kinds of crimes will be happening throughout the United States. Inside terrorism and angry citizens within organizations that want to put in order what they believe should be the rules and foundation of this country. Now I do my research and all, but this is some real life and real time type of shit. As we are going over the hill and coming down it what was once a great neighborhood with some nice ass houses was now a landfill full of port-a-potty type shelters that supposedly offered security and wifi. Out of all of the things on the port-a-potty the part that promoted wifi was the biggest and most noticeable. I got to thinking "What if people's desperation for internet over so called safety is what exposes them to more danger in a landfill full of port-a-potties that are tightly secured and letting out massive amounts of wifi signals in a neighborhood that was once very nice and affluent? Why would people even stay in these when we are told to evacuate the whole town of Manhattan, Kansas aka Wild City, Kanziss? What the fuck is really going on?"……………………………………………………*

Shirtless At The Malls & A Prank Y'ALLS--- *So for some reason I am shirtless coming into the Manhattan Mall from the back doors though. I am sweaty and in a rush and I have to take a* *piss so badly. As I'm entering the mall I'm seeing a lot of White people staring at me in amazement and some in disgust. It's funny though because after entering from the second set of doors that's when this little blonde White girl being around 4 or 5 years old was just staring at me and walking and I had to jump on the wooden bench close to us and hop over her as she just turned her head, but kept moving her body forward and probably walked into that bench as these younger White guys were cracking up, but I didn't look behind me becasue I was in such a rush to get to the restroom. Then for some reason or somehow I ended up in the Topeka WestRide Mall. I don't know when or how, but I'm here. I'm walking into this store that is like a family fun house type of setting except for the fact that it's not a house, it's a big ass store that could be half or one third of the size of a warehouse. As once again there are so many White families and I get the same looks, some stares in amazement and some in disgust as my shirt is still off. As I'm waiting behind people in a line that's going by pretty fast that's when I get up to the counter and I'm asked what it is that I need and I tell the White guy behind the counter "I just need to use the restroom real bad!" That's when he looked at me and then the Spanish feezy beside him behind the counter with him and that's when he grabbed a bag or two and came from around the counter to come up to me and this fool is tall as fuhh up close. That's when he hands me this plastic bag with a light blue shirt in it and another bag with some gifts in it and that's when I just held both of the bags elbow level and I looked at the Spanish feezy behind the counter as she's looking at me and that's when I said "I don't think this fool understood what I was saying, but I'mma head to the restroom." That's when that Spanish feezy looked at me, then that White guy, then she laughed. So I walked away and into a bathroom as many people were lined up, but all I could see were White women with their daughters. I looked at them and they looked at me and we were both giving off awkward looks and awkward energy. As soon as I got to where I could walk in the restroom I could see that this was the womens and girls restroom. I'm power walking to get the fuhh out of here before it looks super weird when this was clearly an accident. The cool thing about this restroom was how the stalls were made from blue painted brick and they were back to back stalls. The labeling around this place is ridiculous though because all it said was "RestRooms," but I only see the women and girls. As I walked out of the restroom and into this big hallway with beautiful blue carpet of all shades that's when I could somehow hear those 2 employees behind the counter speaking loudly. The Spanish feezy says to that White fool "Why did you cheat on me?! Was it because I worked so much all of the time and took care of our daughter and you got close to that one bitch?!" Then that's when I heard that tall White guy say "Huh?! What are you talking about?" Then that's when that Spanish feezy says "I already know about it! You don't have to lie or play stupid!" Then I was thinking "Dizzamn! This must be super serious for them to not only be arguing so loudly that I could hear them from their counter to this hallway, but for them to be talking about it while at work while parents and little kids sign up and pay to play here. Then that's when that Spanish feezy says to the White fool "I hope you thought it was worth it. To lose your family over some easy ass that gives it to everyone else. I even brought her here!" But before she could even fully finish that sentence that's when the White fool says "I'm sorry! It wasn't worth it! I didn't mean to." That's when that Spanish feezy then says "Huh? What?! It was a prank." Then that's when that tall White fool gets quiet and right after he said "Well.......I was pranking you t...." That's when he got…………………………..*

Cheating, Where Are We? And Drown Creek--- *So it's my maintain, her baby daddy, their son, and me all on the porch of my maintain and I's new house. We finally got our house and we love it! Nice and big, green and white painted, nice and fairly new, and for a cheap price. We're all on the porch and I asked my maintain's son if he was ready to go to his dad's house and he responded with "Yes." Although I think he just said that since his dad was here on the porch with us. This little fool has more fun with his mom and I than he does at his dad's house. Then as I see my maintain talking to her baby daddy that's when her baby daddy makes some remarks that were slick and sounded flirtatious towards my maintain. I looked at my maintain and she's smiling at this fool as she's leaned up on the railing by the door. That's when her baby daddy walked up close to my maintain and they started hugging one another and swaying side to side with an overly friendly hug. That's when they then kissed and that's when I yelled and I walked aggressively towards them and I shoved that fool so hard that he had gone through the glass door and the front door to my maintain and I's house so fast that nothing broke. It's literally as if he literally went right through them like some kind of magic trick or a ghost. That's when his son screamed "Daddy!" And ran to the front door and pulled the glass door open and the front main door and ran inside to see if his dad was alright. That's when I had gotten in my maintain's face and I got to yelling "You're seriously going to do this shit right in front of me? Or in general? What the fuck?! We just bought this place too! We're fucking done! FUCK YOU!" Then that's when I looked at our house and I stepped off of the porch as she desperately followed behind me. I'm walking off into the dirt dirt driveway and onto the dirt road. My maintain that is now my ex is still following behind me, pleading for me to forgive her and not to break up with her, but I'm done. I don't care if we had just bought a new place. You don't do me like that! As I'm walking up the road and I see one of the fools I grew up with in Flint Hills Place that's been working at the Manhattan Wal-Mart for some years now named Mickett. He's walking down the dirt road that takes you out of town, so basically one of the main roads and I stopped him to ask him "Is this still considered Manhattan?" That's when he looked around and he said "Yeah. This is still Manhattan." Then that's when I said to him "Dizzamn! Well it's good seeing you my daw. We live out here now. For the time being." Then that's when my maintain had made some weird grunt noise and I walked away as my maintain which is now my ex continued to follow behind me. I walk towards the bridge and I see a steady stream of water even with the excessive rocks and cement slabs that were lodged into the creek. I'm looking at the water and there's something about the stream and the tunnel under this bridge that's attention grabbing. It's as if some lady with a shexy voice is not only speaking to me, but she's singing to me as well. As I continuously stare at the water and the tunnel that's when a couple of these old grey afro'd White ladies say to me "A lot of Army men and men that aren't go in this creek and drown themselves." When they said that it scared me because these elderly women came out of nowhere. My ex maintain is still beside me as I gave her a dirty ass look of disgust. Then that's when those elderly White women preceded by saying "When those bodies are found you can still see oxygen bubbles slowly seep out of their lungs. No one really knows why so many guys choose this place to end it all and why drowning is the preferred way to go." That's when I looked at those 2 elderly women then to the water and the bridge and………………………...*

Old White Lady & The Cops--- So I'm in this huge house where I was hired by this old White lady that told me I was required to wear all black in the cleaning of her house. After about two and a half to about 3 good hours of cleaning up her nice big house and I'm bringing one of the bags down the steps that's when that old White lady with her curly grey afro hair was at the front door with 3 cops with her as she point at me and the 4 of them look at me as I'm totally confused coming down her staircase slowly and that's when…………………………..

Wiz Spar--- So I'm in this MMA cage a few feet away from the rapper Wiz Khalifa. This fool is ripped and looks so much more athletic and healthier. I commend this fool for his total lifestyle change and dedication for not only rapping, but for fighting as well. He's sitting on the floor of the cage as the bell rings and he gets back up ready for another round as he's tall as fuhh with these ripped, but lanky arms and legs and that's when he gets in his stance and puts his hands up and comes in closer to the middle of the ring and…………………………………………...

The Angry Old Dub Dub--- I'm walking into this old antique store to get some classic things that go with the era of my 1971 Chevy Caprice. I've heard about this shop for some time now, but just now making the time to actually check it out. As I walked into the shop that's when I could hear loud talking and no one at the counter. I came into the store more towards the direction of the talking just to make sure that the store is still open and to let them know that they have a customer in their store. The talking gets louder and louder and I end up hearing it being an argument. It's this old ass dub dub yelling at this little White boy who I'm going to assume is her grandson and that's when she yells out at him while gripping his arm tightly and says "YOU LOOK JUST LIKE YOUR DAD! SO SHUT THE FUCK UP!!!!!!"……………………………………

That Yellow Bar--- So I'm in this warehouse that makes a lot of train equipment. I must have decided to finally leave my last job or something because just the sound of this job, the importance, and the equipment all around me looks super expensive. I look around and all that grabs my attention continuously is this long ass yellow bar that is high above the ground and I can't tell if it's metal or not. There's something about this fucking bar that I can't keep my eyes off of and it's as if I'm in a trance and I'm being pulled closer and closer towards this bar until the bar comes loose on one end and the bar is coming in towards my face and I'm trying to move, but…………………………………………..

That Stitched Ass Hole--- So I'm at my ex in-laws for the simple fact of my kids and rearranging the whole living situation custody wise. I'm in my ex's room that passed away as I'm putting up my bags and getting ready to go to sleep since I had to wake up super early to drive from my hometown of Wild City, Kanziss to the capital city of Topeka, Kansas to get on the AmTrak to get to Chicago, Illinois of course. While I'm putting up my bags and preparing to get some sleep so that I can finally rest from the resisting rest on the train, that's when my ex momster in law quietly came into the room where I was staying in a light pink and very thin nightgown that was very high above her knees. I jumped back and put my hands up because I was not expecting for anyone to creep up on me like that. I said "Dizzamn! You scared me!" And that's when she smiled and leaned up on the dresser beside the room door. She gave me *this eye glare like somewhat of a seductive look and she leaned off of the dresser and said something along the lines of the surgery she had. Then she turned around and I just automatically without even thinking said something about how fat her ass looks and it looked so good. That's when she chuckled as I continued to stare and she slowly lifted up her nightgown showing more and more leg until she pulled her nightgown over her ass and her ass looked so good that was until she had spread her ass cheeks open and I saw an ass hole with strings all in and around it as her ass hole was stitched and I was not expecting that sight at all and I jumped back and said "Oh shit! OH shit. Oh SHIT! I forgot that you had that surgery. I forgot that they had to close up your ass hole. As she pulled her nightgown back down and turned back around to face me. That's when she smiled as if she was not embarrassed of my reaction to her stitched up ass hole. Then that's when I say "So that means that you have a shit bag too right?" That's when she lifted up her nightgown on her side and showed me her shit bag that was full of shit and it honestly looked as if it was the plastic bags full of beef from Taco Bell that we had to cut open and pour into the metal pans when I worked there. What went through my head when I saw that was "When she's getting fucked from the back does the person behind her ignore the stitched up ass and is the shit bag placed on the side of her on the bed sloshing around in the bag?"..*

Tonny Tonn--- *I'm in this gym working out hard core in Colorado. People always talk about the elevation change coming from Kansas and whatnot, but guess what?! That has never bothered me. I love the atmosphere and the scenery and mountains every single time I come out here. My training has been ridiculously going more intense for the past year as my goals and dream setting has been taken into a frazy progression for improvement of my health, mindset wise and physically. My motivation, dedication, and commitment has been off the charts with realizing how much I can achieve and be. So anyways, as I'm working out I see this short Mexican feezy from about 12 or so feet from me on this machine with this older White feezy by her that I'm going to assume is her personal trainer from the position that she's at and the instructions that she's giving. I'm amazed at the training tactics they are using and how intense it is for this short little fit Mexican feezy, but the way that she's still going through with it is really impressive. Now whenever I'm working out I'm usually so zoned out that nothing else matters and no one else matters, but the way that she's working out is so impressive to me that I'm zoned out watching her and not really even aware that I'm staring at her until her personal trainer and the Mexican feezy turn around and look at me and they waved and that's when I waved and turned around to get back to my work out because I was a little bit caught off guard and embarrassed. As I'm going back to my machine and my work out I am tapped on my shoulder a few seconds later to see that short Mexican feezy and that White lady that was her personal trainer smiling at me so I paused my music and gave them the headnod to signify my "What's excellent?" To them. That's when they both smiled and that Mexican feezy put her hand out and they said "It's nice to finally meet you, Nappy Vereen!" Then that's when I gave them a look of "Do I know y'all?" And that short Mexican feezy said "Yeah! From GramInsta. We follow each other and I love all of your pictures and videos you post!" That's when I realized who she was and right before I could even say her name, that's when she said "Tonny Tonn." And I said "Dizzamn! What are the chances! I knew you looked super familiar! This is frazy!" That's when Tonny Tonn and her* *personal trainer both looked at me and smiled and they moved in super close to me with their beautiful eyes and they said…………………………*

Stay Here Supervision--- *So I'm at this security guard company called "Stay Here Supervision" applying for a job. Why this place though? Well, because I heard that this place has a high turnover rate and I'm looking at the opportunity within and taking advantage of the people not wanting to keep a job for long. With being in this company I can move up in the ranks faster, get bigger raises, have a greater resume, etc. I've heard that people don't stay here for more than 6 months at a time because of the bullshit they have to go through and the dangerous people and the dangerous calls they have to deal with. As I'm being interviewed already knowing that I'm going to get this job that's when the office door is being kicked in and 4 masked guys come into the office with guns drawn out on us and gunshots are fired at the owner of the company and everything is slow-mo as I'm looking at the guys right before they point their guns at me and that's when………………………………………………...*

Bank Set Up--- *So I'm at this bank about to make a major deposit from a great deal and hustle that I've made with my shirts, books, and my music. Great things have been happening and kind of in a faster way than I expected, but I'm going to embrace the process either way and appreciate all of what I've been through and what I have gone through. I'm legit and I never feel uncomfortable about going to certain places especially the bank, but this day I felt extremely weird because, I don't know….maybe it was the fact that I had so much money this time for a deposit that is substantially higher than most deposits that I make. People, especially bank workers are looking at me, giving me a weird ass vibe that is so noticeable that it's making me feel as if I'm the one doing something wrong. I can feel my energy change, my movement, and even my posture shift as I'm walking towards any open bank teller to deposit my money. I'm feeling as if everything is going by in slow-mo and the bank tellers are moving away further and further from me as I'm getting my money out of my pocket, the money feels a bit different than it usually does. Maybe my hands were wet or maybe I was shaky, but this money felt different from the first time I had touched it and that's when I felt all eyes on me even harder. As I'm going through my pocket to feel the $26,000 is almost irresistible to put into my account. I keep walking towards this bank teller although it feels as if I've already walked about a mile towards them and my mind is telling me no, but I……………………………………………...*

The Museum Train--- *So I'm in this nice ass museum somewhere within this huge beautiful city of Chicago, Illinois. I'm being walked around by this beautiful ass Black woman that's the tour guide giving me lots of noticeable information about the pictures on the wall with the origin and the creators of the pics. Yuh, everything in this museum is nice and beautiful to look at, but the tour guide is the most appealing and I know she looks good and I look good and she knows that I look good too. She's giving me looks and I'm giving her looks and we are slowly walking by each painting and sculpture that was until this taller, darker, and more muscular Black guy tags along with us and he's trying to spit game to the tour guide now because we all know how good she looks. There are a lot of other people in this museum that have their tour guides, but none of them look like this one. Dizzamn! Anyways, this new fool is trying to spit game to our tour guide and she's lightly brushing it off as if she doesn't like it, but we all know that she likes* *the attention. So as this fool is coming through and acting as if he's going to take my shine and opportunity from me that's when I start picking up my game even more to where right before we turned the corner I pulled my tour guide with me into this closet, just her and I and I took no time into my intention and I pulled her clothes off as she helped me and she jumped into my arms and I held her up as I began fucking her and she gripped me tight as I started slamming her down more and more on my dick as she's moaning and feeling good and I'm sucking her chocolate nice nipples as she's holding onto me tighter and tighter and she's breathing and moaning so shexy that I have to hold back from cumming already because it's turning me on more and more with each and every second and each and every stroke. I then pull her off of me and I bend her over quickly grabbing her fat ass and good looking hips and aimed my dick right for that shexy pussy and I slid my dick right into her pussy from behind as her and I both let out this sigh and sound of goodness and I began grabbing both of her ass cheeks tightly and pulled her body in close to mine so her pussy could take in all of my dick and then I pushed her away, then pulled her in, pushed her back, and pulled her in repeatedly just pounding her pussy and feeling how great her skin and ass is and how wet she is on the inside. As she's arching her back and I'm pounding this pussy as if I'm trying to prove a point to her as if this is the best she ever had and the one she'll only want. She feels so good inside and out and she sounds so good too. As I'm pounding this pussy so good that's when I almost told her that I loved her and this pussy until the closet door opened and my tour guide ran off of my dick which felt so good and she ran to her clothes to cover up her body that looks better than her clothes, but it was that fool that was with us in the tour looking as if he had missed out in some good action, opportunity, and some good pussy. That fool shuts the closet door behind him and he drops his pants and takes his shirt off and the rest of his clothes and this fool is ripped! Might even be a little more ripped than me, but I'm not totally sure because I see myself on the regular. This fools dick is out and already hard and I looked down at my dick knowing that my dick is big and I know my dick is big because plenty of feezies have told me, but this fool was packing unless I see my dick everyday and I don't notice how much bigger it is than others do. As I look down at my dick it is literally hanging down lower by strings that is my pubic hair and a paddle like sort of thing and that tour guide says "No strings attached? What you see is what you hit!" As the buff Black fool moves in closer towards our tour guide and picks her up and turns her around that's when he bent her over and he shoves his dick in her as her eyes got all big and she grabbed my dick and pulled me in closer to her face I thought to myself "Fuck! I always said I would never run a train on a feezy cuz that would be weird." But this tour guide looked so good and I needed to bust this nut to make it official that I smashed this feezy that looked so good. So as she's moaning and keeping her mouth open I pulled in closer to put my dick in her wet mouth and it felt so good as she's moving back and forth with the force of the guy behind her I began moaning as the inside of this tour guides mouth felt as good as her pussy did, but then the fool behind her started breathing heavily and moaning which threw me off so I looked down at the tour guide while my dick was down her throat and I grabbed her head and started jamming my dick in and out of her mouth so that I could hear her gagging and moaning over everything else and that's when I felt my body shaking and the tour guide moaning louder and louder and that's when something was brought up about paying taxes by our tour guide and…………………………………*

Back At "The Press"--- So here I am back at my last job before my current, Ag Press. The place I worked at for years that is definitely one of my favorite jobs I've ever worked at. As I'm at my machine running some book that is displaying some things about some event that's happening within the next month. After watching my machine run out that's when I see "The Top Dog" aka The Eye Browed Wizard aka the shop manager walk by and just inspecting the area micromanaging the area/shop. My machine runs out of paper and I write my count down on my progress sheet and my time and then I walked to the office near my machine and Bornie was in there on her computer and Ruthless was in there on her computer and I went over next to Bornie to her phone to pick it up and dial a number as Bornie looked over at me and……………………

My Minds Already Made Up--- So here I am in my Caprice driving towards the KC downtown area. My fool, well one of the fools that use to be my fools lives in the KC area and although I cut this fool off for him being a fake ass friend and there being a numerous amount of times that he's done me wrong, but he doesn't think he has simply because I kept letting this fool get away with it. Some way somehow he messages me knowing that I'm headed towards KC which I'm pretty sure it's from maybe his maintain or our mutual friends on my BaceFook page. Although before I had blocked this fool he was supposedly going to come to Wild City to talk to me one on one and face to face my mind had already been made up about cutting this fool off because there's just way too many examples that I can provide this fool for when, why, and how he has done me wrong and has not been a good friend. Although my mind is already made up I decided to meet up with this fool at the address he messaged me to hear what he has to make up…..so I made it to this fools house and he greets me in to the backyard and he has this plastic fishing pole with a magnet on the bottom while he's on the red porch. This fool Timptation asks me "So why did you block me bro? I was planning on seeing you down there to talk about the stuff we needed to talk about." That's when I lightly laughed and I said "I blocked you because I kept coming up with more and more times of when you had no loyalty or respect for me. On top of the numerous other times I had already listed." That's when Timptation then says "My intentions were to never make you feel like I wasn't a good friend." That's when I then say "Your actions proved otherwise my daw. Just about everyone I had a problem with or had a problem with me for some reason you ended up being cool with those fools. I told you why I don't fuck with them and gave you valid reasons, but you act like you stuck up for me, but you end up being cool with them because even the fools that don't fuck with me can see how fake and vulnerable you are and end up bringing you to their side. I'm good my daw, there's really nothing you can say to me to convince me otherwise." Then that's when this fool tries bringing up other excuses that aren't valid for how and why he has been a good friend and I'm not even trying to hear it because out of his weak ass 3 excuses they don't even match up or compare to my reasonings and my examples. Then as he's still fake fishing with that plastic magnetic fishing pole that's when his maintains son comes out of the back door to the backyard and he asks Timptation about something I could barely understand and that's when I walked towards the end of the red back porch and I said to Timptation "My minds already made up my daw. You have a good one." As I stepped off the porch and…………………………..

Practicing My Punches--- *So here I am outside on a sidewalk of Bluemont Avenue in my hometown of Manhattan, Kansas aka Wild City, Kanziss practicing my cardio and my boxing punches. I'm in my boxing stance as I practice my jabs along with my combos working my technique and shoulders and creating a scenario in my head as if I'm performing in an actual ring and making sure my arms are tight to my body and face and that's when…………………………..*

Scraping Ink--- *So uh, here I am in the department of screen print at my job. Frazy thing though is that I'm not running any shirts as I am scraping ink from the squeegees and whatnot. I'm back from my trip in Illinois and apparently while I was gone somehow the workers here had mixed so many ink colors onto multiple squeegees that already had colors on them which I don't know how that was even done or allowed when everyone in this department has been here for over 2 years and they know to not even do anything that doesn't even make such sense. So more people including myself are scraping ink off of squeegees instead of running the presses and knocking out shirt orders. This is ridiculous, but we're getting paid by doing some of the easiest work anyone can do so no complaints. I'm just really confused as to why and how this happened? It's almost as if management isn't so tight when I'm gone, but they are when I'm here. So as I'm scraping ink from the squeegees I noticed someone new working here that I have not seen since my 8th grade year at Eisenhower Middle School. Her name, Cortknee. She's this blonde dub dub that's always had these big ass cheeks whether she was smiling or not. She comes by my trash can and begins scraping ink and she's talking to me as if she is trying to get to know me which is funny because she doesn't even know yet that we already met one another. So we're talking about how long we have been working here, our previous jobs, where we are from, and whatnot and before I was going to tell her that I knew her from middle school that's when Ginger Snap my manager of this department came up to us to tell me that we had to be 6 feet apart although there was no more mask wearing and that I was able to run my machine now. I thought to myself "I swear they are only paying attention to us whenever I'm here." So I told Cortknee that it was nice talking to her as I walked over to my press and I was taking my time to set up my squeegees and that's when……………………………………...*

The Spending Bending Vending Machine--- *So I'm at this hospital or emergency type of facility where I'm walking by the waiting room and I see 2 fools I know sitting in these 2 chairs right next to the room that has the vending machine, drinks, etc. The 2 fools I see are Loc-Tee and ForeDread. We all look at one another and give each other the head nod to basically say "What's excellent?" to one another and acknowledge that we see one another. I walked into that room and dizzamn! I was not expecting to see some futuristic type of shit like this. Now I don't drink soda, but this soda machine was nice! So nice that it makes the soda look so good from the photo and the machine was so convincing with the detail and the lights that I could almost see why people would drink soda. This might sound weird, but this soda machine looks shexy and it goes hard. Then I looked over at the vending machine next to it which had nice green flashing lights on it with a scanner to scan your credit or debit card and lights so bright on the machine highlighting the products. As I'm looking at the selections that's when I heard the vending machine make a noise and a claw like arm came out from the top of the vending machine from within and began spinning and I was thinking to myself "I didn't even enter in my* selection yet. Can this machine read my mind too?" As the claw went all the way to the bottom of the machine it had picked up a Reese's Cup and picked it up and grabbed it and put it back in the place where the rest of the Reese's Cups were. I looked at this machine in awe because this machine was so advanced and sophisticated that whenever someone forgets to pick up their change or forgets their selection the machine picks it back up and waits for another person to make a selection. I wondered about if this machine had other sensors or cameras and then………………………

Unbreakable Icy DriveWay--- So it's icy as fuhh outside! So cold here in the Midwest Manhattan, Kansas aka Wild City, Kanziss. I'm in this neighborhood where it is almost hard to even consider it a neighborhood because there are barely any houses on this big plot of land. My neighbor is across the driveway and she's this fit dub dub that has a shaved head and she owns her own fitness facility. She was telling me earlier about how the ice in our driveways are unbreakable and that if I was able to break through it all with my sledge hammer that she would publish me and give me an unlimited membership at her gym. So here I am with my sledge hammer in my driveway thinking about how this ice looks so thin and breakable and how her challenge is accepted by me. As I looked over at her house and then my driveway that's when I began slamming my sledge hammer heavily into the icy driveway seeing it crack as I picked my sledge hammer back up and slammed it into the ground with powerful force feeling like John Henry with each and every powerful slam into the ground. I see the ice crack more and more as I get louder with each and every powerful slam into the ground. I was slamming so loud and letting out so much noise that I knew my neighbor had to have heard me along with the distant neighbors too. As I slammed my sledge hammer more and more into the icy driveway that's when all of the ice had broken through and I fell through the driveway about 4 feet just to land onto my driveway again, but this time there was no ice. No ice at all! In, on, or around my driveway. I'm looking around and there's no ice or snow anywhere to be seen. It's as if it's not even winter anymore. Did I break the ice that was supposedly unbreakable to shift the seasons or did I work on the ice breaking for so long that I worked throughout the whole season?...........................

That Dog--- I'm in some junk yard of some sort except there is no junk. There's only grass and a barbwire fence with even more barbwire on top of the fence rolled around it as this big ass light brown mixed with dark brown dog is viciously chasing after me as I'm running so fast from my adrenaline rushing and my survival instincts kicking in as I'm getting closer and closer to the fence as the dog is getting closer and closer to me and that's when……………………………...

Mall Piss--- So I'm in the Manhattan Mall either coming in from the front doors or leaving the first restaurant on the left inside of the mall and I have to take a serious piss. I'm power walking through all sorts of people with their babies in their strollers as this is urgent. And then that's when……....I'm coming in from the entrance part of the Manhattan Mall again as I'm power walking through people again and I'm in such a hurry that I'm not even slowing my pace down. My attitude is that these people better move out of my way because this is such an emergency that I'm willing to plow through any and everyone until I can finally take my piss. As I'm walking through White people and Asian people with their babies in their strollers that's when I see *these 2 tall Black guys dressed fresh in black and red and they see this short buff tatted Black guy come their direction as they moved, but not with much space or time and within the process that's when I still wasn't slowing down and I stepped on the tip of one of the tall Black guys shoes to the right of me and I cringed in the process which that's a violation, but once again while in the process of needing to piss so badly all I really allowed myself to do was look over my shoulder briefly and say "I'm sorry!" as I kept my power walking pace. I walked past where Hat World used to be and I walked past a mall security guard and I then reversed and saw the doors that said "Employees Only," but I didn't give a fuhh due to this urgent situation. Although I could get into trouble and be kicked out of the mall I really didn't give a fuhh at this point. As I'm walking through I see some people come out from their backdoors and they're looking at me as I obviously am not allowed back here, but nothing is being said to me verbally. As the White couple from Foot Locker pass me that's when I see this Asian couple give me a look of "What the fuck are you doing back here?!" as well. As I followed the Asian couple because it was in here where I remembered I didn't need to take these hallways to reach the nearest restroom which I thought for some reason was at the other end of the mall. As I'm following this Asian couple as they are about to go through some doors that take you near the entrance of the mall I had came from and outside of Hat World that's when I had power walked even faster to the doors to get ahead of them which they had even given me a stronger "What the fuck?!" face until they had seen that I was opening the doors for them. That's when they had given me a big huge smile on their faces and said "Thank you, thank you, thank you." very lightly and that's when I could see a mall security guard outside of the doors as he saw me helping this Asian couple bring their big metal cart of food through the doors so nothing was mentioned about me being in the "Employees Only" hallway. As that Asian couple had completely pulled through that's when I let the door close behind me and I focused on the closest restroom which is a few feet from where I am at now and past the food court and that's when……………………...*

Optimistic OKC Sign--- *I was going through abandoned junk earlier and that's when I found an abandoned or thrown out OKC sign that was in decent condition. This sign is just needing a little bit of fixing up and that's exactly what I was going to do with it or at least replicate it and try my best to duplicate it with another sheet of paper and some markers. So here I am now invited to a mutual friend of mine from the gym I would work out at and through BaceFook named Mathis Reading's house as we were invited over for the Super Bowl which of course we are going for the Chiefs to win. As it's half time I'm with my sheet of paper and brown, orange, and blue markers doing my best to duplicate this OKC Travels poster with this smiling middle aged White couple with "OKC" in blue and bold right above their heads and a downtown that looked nothing like the downtown we had seen when we had gone there with an ocean and the beach behind them. Some things were very misleading in this poster, but aye I'm just trying to make it look good at this point. As I'm sketching as precisely as I can on my copy so that I can flip the image and make some money off of it, that's when my maintain who is sitting on the chair across from the table I'm drawing this picture on looks at me and says "Just leave the picture alone. If you ask me I'd say you're just wasting your time trying to draw up what's going to take up so much time and not even look nearly as good as it should." That's when Mathis Reading and his wife looked over at me like "Dizzamn!" but they only said that with their eyes and that's when I looked at my maintain and I said "You need to be more optimistic. The least I can do is* *try and say at least I did it." That's when my maintain had looked at me as if I had insulted her in the worst way as Mathis Reading and his wife looked at me as if I had fucked up and then…………………………...*

<u>That Cost At Ross---</u> *So I'm with my maintain, her mom, along with myself as we enter the Ross in my maintain and I's hometown of Manhattan, Kansas aka Wild City, Kanziss. I'm guessing we had decided to go here just to do some looking around because we weren't very specific about what we were going to do or look around for at the store. As we leave the parking lot and we approach the door to the Ross store that's when we all…………………………*

<u>The Tunnel Of Bones---</u> *So here I am underneath this bridge within a tunnel with my daw Rickardo and his blonde dub dub maintain which I swore they had broken up and stopped talking. Why are we here? We're here because we wanted to figure out if it was trueness about there being dead body's in the river that flows underneath this bridge and through this tunnel. As we are in this water this is about 2 to 2 and a half feet at the most on us that's when we began shoveling so much water that after an hour or two of digging we had caused the water to flow around us due to the amount of dirt and sand we had dug up and put around us plus with certain spots of this water being so much shallower than the others spots. As we have dug up more and more, that's when our shovels had began making clunking and clanking noises as if we had been hitting tough spots of cement or maybe even rocks. Prior to that I did notice how Rickardo had backed up from the shoveling as his maintain and I had done the majority of the digging. As we put our shovels down that's when Rickardo's maintain and I had gotten down on our hands and knees and began digging up the rest of the dirt and we came across bones. Human bones. A human skeleton. Arm bones, hip bones, and skulls. Rickardo's maintain and I had looked at one another like "Wow! What the fuhh?! So what we heard wasn't fake!" We had hit a jackpot as this is huge and going to be even bigger news for our town. We then both looked at Rickardo as this fool is acting super weird now as he's pacing back and forth and acting nervous as fuhh and that's when he…………………………………..*

<u>The Shoe Store---</u> *So I'm in this shoe store. I'm not sure if it's an actual shoe store or if it's a shoe department within a bigger store. As I'm in my red tank top looking and feeling big as fuhh as I'm going through each aisle looking for good products with good prices and good deals. The kids section is where I'm actually at to be exact looking for new stuff for the kids. As I walk past the hoodies, coats, and pants and over to the shoes that's when I see a white pair of shoes for girls with a paint splash design on them. A pink, light blue, and a neon yellowish green paint splash. These look like a good fit for my daughter. As I walk towards the shoes and I take them out the box to hold them and see them up closer that's when I see my daw Donjel walk by while on his cell phone and I was gonna give this fool the "What's excellent?!" head nod, but he gave me this fucked up look and he walked right past me as if he doesn't fuck with me, didn't know or recognize me, or didn't want me to say shit to him. I felt offended and disrespected so I didn't want to assume shit so put the shoes back in the box and followed the direction of this fool and that's when he was in the aisle across next to some cart with some feezy by it that I recognized after I had noticed that………………...*

<u>Photog In Flint Hills Place---</u> *I had no idea that this photographer that I have on my GramInsta named Kelly K. lived in section 8 Flint Hills Place in Manhattan, Kansas up until now. Here the fuhh we are meeting for the first time unexpectedly as we cross paths looking at one another as we definitely noticed one another as we………………………………..*

<u>The David Goggins & Martin Lawrence Movie---</u> *So here I am in a movie role that is historical in my eyes. My break through! My big break! I'm playing a part in a serious comedy movie with not only Martin Lawrence, but one of the biggest motivational speakers of this generation, David Goggins. Who would have ever guessed or imagined to see him in a big movie theatre? But with the buzz of his name and how he has risen to popularity and fame in a way I'm not surprised that HollyWood has put him in this movie called* **"Embrace The Suck!"** *In this movie comedian Martin Lawrence is being trained to handle adversity better and to become a world class fighter and Olympian along with dealing with real life situations. He has come across David Goggins on social media and reached out to him to help him train to be a tougher individual and become better with his relationships and to pull himself from out of the trenches to be as tough or even tougher than David Goggins. Throughout the movie little did they know that they started rubbing personalities off of one another slowly and the roles started to reverse. That'll be later on through the movie though. For now we are in the scene where David Goggins has convinced Martin Lawrence to go to the zoo and now they are in the tank swimming with the polar bears as Martin Lawrence is panicking as 2 polar bears swim around them and David Goggins is surrounded as well, but calm with his shirt off in the ice cold water as everyone from the concession stands next to the tank where I am at is watching and people below on the sidewalk are watching too. As I walked around a corner and lots of White people are by as they see 3 Black guys in this polar bear section, 2 in the pool, and one which is myself around the corner getting undressed as I'm ready to jump in the pool too as this one blonde dub dub looks at me smiling asking "You're not going to swim with the polar bears too are you?" That's when I pulled my shorts down while my dick and balls had shown and she smiled hugely and that's when I pulled my boxers back up, but the rest of my shorts down and she smiled again and that's when she said "Don't die on me. I wanna talk to you after!" That's when I went in for the kiss and she licked all over my face and in my mouth and started sucking on my tongue then my neck and my nipples then started to go down low until I had to pull her off and I told her to hold on for that. As I stepped back from her and I looked at the polar bear tank while David Goggins looks very serious and Martin Lawrence is still panicking although the polar bears aren't near him and he's floating in the water and not drowning that's when I locked in and I began running towards the polar bear tank full force and as I'm getting closer and closer and getting ready for my leap that's when I slipped on a patch of water and what went from full force running has turned into………………………………………………………*

<u>BrickTown Parking---</u> *So here I am again. Well, here WE are again! My family and I are out here in Oklahoma City, Oklahoma in BrickTown for some event or concert this time. We had taken 2 separate vehicles as my maintain is in some newer white car with our oldest son with her and I'm in the van with our youngest son with me. We could have all fit in the van or the car, but for some reason we decided to split up. Who knows? Maybe while out here in OKC we planned on picking up a lot of stuff and bringing it back to Manhattan, Kansas aka Wild City,*

Kanziss once we're done here. As my maintain had left to find parking somewhere else that's when I began driving by the baseball stadium, but there's parking over here and last time I was here which was a year ago there was no parking except for only statues and bricks before the entrance into these places. As I'm cruising slowly by all of these spots that are parked in that's when I drove over the sidewalk and I saw this parking lot security/maintenance orange truck parked next to the restrooms. I say out loudly to myself and my son in the backseat in his carseat "Hold on!" As I creeped up behind the parked orange truck that no one was behind and I parked behind it as I'm looking around and I got a little paranoid because I don't want the maintenance man to not even think about someone being parked behind him and he backs up into the van or for us to get ticketed for being parked right here. So I put the van back in reverse and as I pulled back a little bit then put my van back into drive that's when I pulled up between the orange maintenance truck and the restrooms as tightly as I could then put the van back in park as I turned the van off and I looked around for a little bit and that's when....................

Working For A Rainy Day--- *I don't even know when, where, or why, but my whole department of coworkers is outside in what seems to be a jungle or rainforest in the pouring rain. When I say "The Pouring Rain" I mean it's raining so hard that it almost makes us flinch and our eyes red and blurry and hard to see. We are drenched in our clothes and everything we have with us is soaked. If you have water proof of anything especially your phone then you're in luck, but then again with this rain you would almost second guess if your phone would be waterproof enough. It's raining so hard and heavy that there is barely any talking as we are just following one another as closely as we can until we at least reach a hut that most of us could gain shelter if possible. I'm so confused to how we ended up in the deep forest as I know this can't be in Kansas because none of the woods look like this and I don't think Kansas has any of these exotic looking trees or these animals either. Unless we are in some kind of huge zoo rainforest portion or something. We continue to walk forward in this line in the hopes of finding anyone or anything that would help us. As the line we are all in slows down that's when I look up ahead the best that I can and I see a group of people underneath this pavilion looking thing with a tin roof and some benches and tables as people are walking up drenched in rain and so soaked as they put a punch sheet into this machine to either punch in or punch out and that's when I looked at them and thought to myself "What the fuhh?! Are we still at work or are we headed to work?" Then that's when my coworker "Big Joke" had turned around and said "Can you believe this stupid shit?! I swear I can't wait to get a new job." That's when I had looked at him in a weird way that probably looked even weirder because of all the rain in my face and because I had no idea that this fool was in front of me the whole time and that's when...........................*

My Mexican Army Friend--- *I'm outside of AggieVille working out and walking with my dumb bells until I was approached on the side by a car that was creeping slow. I thought it was someone trying to be hard and start some shit so I sat my dumbbells down and I stood back up to look at the car as they stopped right next to me I thought to myself once again that they're trying to be hard and start some shit as the car window slowly rolled down and I'm waiting for the action as the dark tinted window slowly rolled down. As my adrenaline is ready to kick in and I'm preparing for anything from shit talking to threats and even guns being pulled out on me.*

As the window is rolling down that's when this Mexican guy that looked very familiar was in his driverseat, but leaned over to the passengers side and he said "Yo! Give me some tips on how to get big as fuck like you! Dude!!" That's when I looked at him and recognized him quickly as he's one of the Army guys that gave me a compliment about how big I was a few months ago when I was outdoors working out with my dumb bells and that's when my anxiety, adrenaline, and tenseness had went away as I busted out laughing and said "Oh shit! What's good my daw! I thought you were gonna be someone else trying to start shit. What's excellent with you though? How you been and what are you up to?" That's when he laughs back and says "Aww, naw dude it's all good. I'm just about to get some food until I saw your big ass and thought I might as well pull up on you and say something." As we both laughed as he pulled up closer to the curb and I walked up to his car and that's when……………………………………………..

Niece In Pantry--- *I'm in the kitchen of my oldest sister's house looking for something to eat. As I walked past the fridge to head straight to the big ass pantry that looks like a closet door that's when I opened the door to see a room full of snacks, but the top rack with my niece laying on the top of it as if it's a bunk bed as she watches a movie on the other side of the pantry and I was so thrown off shocked and surprised that I didn't even say anything I just backed away slowly and shut the door as I…………………………………....*

My Own Wedding Cake & Eat It Too--- *So I'm at my own wedding reception or whatever the fuck this is. I'm fucking confused because I'm next to this red head dub dub that's thick and looks asiago, but I'm not even sure who the fuck she is or how I even met her. I'm at this big table that is a celebration all around us as if we had already gotten married. I'm like the only Black person here being surrounded by so many White people and goofy White guys paying so much attention to me. My bride was the daughter of a cop that was even happy I was marrying his daughter. If he was this happy about me marrying his daughter then I could only imagine how excited he would be if he found out I was long thick dicking her too. I'm not gonna lie though, this setup was nice and was special, but I still don't know how all of this even happened. As this big ass wedding cake is being brought up and a smaller cake as well being brought to our table right in front of my soon to be bride and I and everyone gets excited as my soon to be is clapping loud and smiling and that's when someone yells out "YOU CAN HAVE YOUR OWN WEDDING CAKE AND EAT IT TOO!" As everyone began laughing and my soon to be had cut me out a piece of cake and put it on my plate and I was thinking in my head "I don't even eat cake anymore. Who the fuhh is she and who are these people? How did they get here? How did I get here? What am I even about to do with my life?" As everything slows the fuck down and I'm looking around feeling woozy, dizzy, sick, and everyone is around me laughing and smiling as my soon to be wife grabs my arm and rocks me side to side asking me "Are you asiago?" And that's when I looked at her like "That's my word!" Then Keak Da Sneak's song "That's my word" started playing and then I passed out and……………………………………..*

My Ex Is Stalking Again--- *So I'm in the passenger side of this beat up ass Buick with this grimey looking older White fool in the driver's seat that I'm pretty sure is a scammer and a drug addict. He's watching me as I'm nervously looking around wondering how the fuck I had even got in this car and how I even know this fool. As he continues to look at me as if he's waiting for* *me to answer him I am looking super confused because I seriously don't even know what the fuck this fool had even asked me. As I look around, that's when I said "Let me use the restroom in this gas station right quick and I'll be back." That's when before he could even respond back I had opened the car door and stepped the fuck out because this fool gives me the vibe of not being trusted plus his breath smelt like shit and he was dirty, both looking and charcter wise. I slammed the car door and I looked at the gas station which was a Casey's gas station. I'm walking closer and closer to this gas station as I'm thinking of how the fuck I got here, how the fuck I'm going to get away, and what ideas, plans, or lies I can tell to get me to my comfort zone. I got closer and closer to the gas station door and all I could seriously think about was really taking a piss. I walked into the store to see that this Casey's was more than a gas station. This was a Super Casey's or something, especially with the shops in here, the clothes, food, souvenirs, etc. For a split second I had forgotten that I was in a Casey's gas station while some weird ass White fool was outside being weird about some shit that I ended up with somehow. As I'm walking further and further into this store as I'm looking for any of the restroom signs that's when I see the restroom signs, but then I get distracted by the food that's laid out at this gas station that looks so good. Not only does this Casey's have the good looking hot dogs on the turner, but this Casey's has an all out all you can eat buffet which is a first I've ever seen in a Casey's or any gas station at that, but once I had thought about it and stared at it some more that's when I had thought about how unsanitary that would have to be especially in this shopping portion with the amount of people that come in from state to state and on a daily basis. I continued to walk through and walk by and proceed to head towards the restroom and that's when I had seen her! My red headed ex "J-NO!" The feezy that won't leave me the fuck alone since I left her ass. The feezy that made fake pages and came up with so many creative, but yet entertaining rumors and lies about my maintain and I to make us look bad and to make us break up. Yuh, her! I stopped where I was walking and stood in my place as she continued to stare me down as she walked by staring at me although she had almost ran into a cart of sweets. I'm looking at her and thinking to myself "What are the chances that I see her **shugly** ass here? Does she know that White fool in the car?" Then that's when she cracked a smile at me as I continued to walk towards the restroom and as I opened the restroom door and stepped in that's when I had somehow ended up in this basement house party with red neon lights everywhere as B.I.G.'s song "Big Poppa" was playing loudly with lots of Black people around me, but still a variety of other people as I look around and I'm vibing and enjoying the atmosphere while seeing everyone dance, but as I look around I see this dub dub in the crowd of dancing people just staring at me and not even dancing with the people around her. I had to double look and guess who the fuck it was? Yuh, J-NO! Again! Just staring at me while slowly cracking a smile and that's when she……………………………..*

The Parent Teacher CONference--- *Here I am pulling into the Bluemont Elementary school parking lot except for the mini back parking lot is now on the side of the school nearest to the entrance. I'm parking my white Chevy Impala in the parking lot and getting out to walk right into the front doors of this old school that I had once attended that my kids are now going to. As I entered the building the first thing I had noticed was that there were new steps placed within the building not too far from the front entrance door. I followed the signs that have directions to where the teachers and grades are for my kids. As I follow the signs I'm reminiscing about* *when I had once attended this school and how much has changed. I made it to the classroom for my daughter and I am so thrown off from the amount of faculty in this one room along with who the fuck the faculty is too. Out of all the people in this town I would not have ever expected for the faculty and the people talking about my daughter would be my current coworkers that I know throughout the whole building of my job. It looks like a board meeting or a parole meeting as they're all wrapped around the room as I stepped in. Most of the people in this room don't like me or I have not talked to, so I can only imagine how this is going to go. I take a seat while everyone else in the room is talking and giving me looks and that's when I pull out my phone and I go to my YouTube app and ironically DayLyt is on my newsfeed with a video titled "Parent Teacher Conferences And It's Sick Origin." I clicked it and turned the volume down and DayLyt gets straight to the point about how "Parent Teacher Conferences is a sick sick thing. You leave your kids at home with whoever or whatever while you drive away from your kids to talk about them behind their backs! While all of these pedophiles and sick people keep tabs online and around the school on these events so they have you away from home so while you or your significant other are in a meeting away from home that's when that sick person creeps in." I'm focusing in real close to what he's saying as I'm tapping my finger on the power strip of outlets that goes around the room. I stood up after pausing the video and thought to myself "Although what DayLyt says sometimes is out of control, he does make so much sense at the same time." As the faculty looked at me I had walked out right quickly into the hallway to look out the window to see if I could see my car which I could, but there's some black car parked directly behind it although there are other open parking stalls available. Also, only my car is where there is another car parked behind it which I find pretty weird. That's when I had ran to the office and looked around for the intercom as I picked up the walkie talkie looking thing and pressed the button on the sound board looking thing and the side button on the walkie talkie and I said "Attention. The black car that is parked behind my white Impala could you please move your car please. I repeat, the black car that is parked behind my white Impala in the front parking lot to the right of the school entry doors could you please move your car please." Then that's when I had sat the walkie talkie down not knowing how to turn it off as there was a weird noise making a sound through the intercoms from the walkie talkie. I then look to my left and there's some blonde little White girl about 5 or so in the office with me on a chair just staring at me. I'm looking confused as she's looking at me then the walkie talkie until some White guy comes busting through the door to the office room yelling at me saying "You didn't have to be so fucking rude about my fucking car! I'm moving it now!" Then that's when I look at this fool with my "What the fuhh?! Are you serious right now! I wasn't even being rude!" look. And that's when he…………………………………………………*

Mom On Podcast--- *So I don't know when or how, but I had somehow got my mom to be on an episode of my podcast which to me is always unheard of and unrealistic and so unexpected as my mom doesn't open up about much or admit fault in anything that involves her wrong doings. Maybe this will be her chance to do so and talk about all of the things that she still continues to harbor that only hurts and hinders her. As we met up at this conference room that I had reserved ironically at Bluemont Elementary which is one of the schools I had not only spent so many grades in, but I had also had the most problems in as well. The only cache though is that I had to have my youngest son with me which he doesn't understand instructions and he is* *probably going to be so needy and annoying and pulling my equipment down that it's going to be hard to even have a comfortable conversation or podcast without anxiety and losing track of things and thoughts because of my son. I'm not being negative, I'm just being realistic and speaking from experience. So as we all 3 entered this room I had reserved for this special podcast episode that's when I set up my equipment and positioned my camera angles right from my smart phones and their tripod stands and began the podcast. I can see that my son is looking around at everything as he is just waiting to snatch something as I tell my mom to introduce herself to the camera starting with her name, age, and where she's from. Which she does. She's staring off with a great personality and smiling, but me knowing my mom I know that she has gone through some things in life that still mess with her because she has never fully dealt with them. Then that's when my son tried grabbing one of my phones until I stood up and he just ran off with the box that one of the tripods came in. My mom re-positions the phone that was recording to the left of us, but had us out of the frame which annoyed me because I seriously don't see how she couldn't have noticed that when the camera is pointing in our direction. I try not to look, sound, or be annoyed, but I knew that this shit was going to happen. My son is starting to whine while we are still recording, but I try to ignore it and talk over it all. Then that's when it got to the topic of my grandad passing away and that's when my mom had looked super emotional and I asked "Is it OK if we talk about this? You lost your mom when you were 16. Now you lost your dad. How do you feel?" That's when she had gotten quiet as I could see a tear roll down her face and she says "I don't want to talk about it……………………………...*

Outside Late Talking About The Late--- *So I'm outside on the sand of Milford Lake which us Kansas people call "The Beach." I'm leaning on the side of my 1971 Chevy Caprice while parked on the sand as I'm looking at the lake as the sun slowly looks as if it is slowly dipping itself into the lake waters from afar. It's a beautiful scene as I just look and I think about life as the sun reflects from the waters I reflect on my life that was until these 2 young looking White fools had come up to me and I noticed one of them from when he would hang out with my ex's little brother. He came up to me and gave me the "What's excellent?" head nod and said "Look, I had no idea about your baby mama passing away until…………………………..*

J-Crooks "Lap"Top--- *So I'm in my maintain's mom's car while my maintain is in the passenger side and my momster in law is in the driver's seat and I'm in the backseat. I don't know when, how, or why, but my maintain and her mom were talking about how they stole one of my daws laptops named J-Crook which they are showing me his black laptop which is pretty nice and has a nice keyboard and big screen. They go to his saved files and talk about what they wonder this fool looks up and saves. Which J-Crook is a weird fool so I could only imagine what's going to be saved on his laptop. I know him and I aren't as close as we once were, but I'm hoping they don't see anything that's going to make me look at this fool a lot differently than I already do. As my maintain goes through his saved content she sees a lot of saved files that are porn videos. My maintain's not into porn at all, but with her nosey ass and her nosey ass mom nothings going to stop them as I watch them not knowing much to do or say because what if I find out something about this fool that I, myself, or others don't know much about or nothing about that needs to be known? Who knows what kind of porn this would be. So the porn file is* *opened and it starts a video with this thick dub dub getting on top of this Black guys lap that's on this couch. All you see is a big Black dick and a nice White thick fat ass with some good looking legs as the camera zooms in on her holding his dick straight to go right below her wet pussy right before she lets out that gasp and slides down on it before she wiggles her ass and slowly starts riding and bouncing all over this dick as they are both breathing heavily and the Black guy is smacking her ass. The camera zooms back out and shows more of these 2 porn actors bodies then faces and that's when all of our jaws had dropped because it was my daw J-Crook smashing this White feezy that surprisingly looked good as fuhh as he's known for smashing feezies that aren't even selfie worthy at all. I turned away from the laptop in disgust because I couldn't believe I saw my fools dick and it was bigger than mine. I said "What the fuhh?!!!" As my maintain and her mom were still watching as I looked back at the screen for the doggystyle part and that's when I noticed something about J-Crook's face as he was rocking back and forth with the power thrusts and that's that his face was off centered each time he had moved. This fool J-Crook cropped his fucking face over some other guys face for pleasure to push his porn watching experience to another level. When I had noticed that that's when I yelled out "Do y'all see that that's not even his fucking face?!" That's when they had both looked back at me and they said "How do you know what his "fucking face" looks like?" Then that's when I said "No! That's not even J-Crook!" Then that's when…………………………………………..*

Left Ear's Disease--- *So there's this recording artist that has been dominating the billboards and the charts for the past 10 years named "Left Ear" from Kansas. Yuh, you "heard" me "right!" "Left, Ear" is an artist from Kansas that has soaked up so much knowledge from every region of the United States while being from the middle of the map, Kansas. Left Ear says his name is not only in remembrance of Left Eye, but for "What you have not seen before or you have even heard." This artist is definitely a one of a kind and unique from sounds he hears and the sounds he gives off. A very spiritual guy. This artist has been touring the world and breaking records all while making money and feeling on top of the planet earth that was until one day he had woken up from his bed on his tour bus feeling a migraine he has never felt before as 3 groupies were in the bed with him. He slowly gets up from the left side of his body as he feels his left ear leaking something that at first he thought was sleep slobber or maybe even cum on his pillow from the night before. As he lifts up and touches his left ear he feels a wet oozing substance as he almost panics as he brings his hand back in front of his face to see what looks like ear wax and very dark blood. Blood so dark that it's basically black. He turns around so fast to look at his pillow and sees that there is black blood and wax all over his pillow and now he's panicking while he's getting light headed along with an adrenaline rush as he jumps up from the bed and that's when………………………………………...*

It's Going Down...Town Topeka--- *So here the fuck I am on a business trip with my coworker Dani in the capital city of Topeka, Kansas. Now, I used to be in the boys home with people from Topeka and I've been to Topeka a numerous amount of times and this time is being accounted for as well. Now Topeka is the capital of Kansas, but it has been getting worse and worse. From all of the cities I have been to I would say that Saint Louis has some of the roughest looking areas, but downtown Topeka has been looking more and more like Saint Louis especially around the downtown area with more and more businesses leaving to go elsewhere* *due to Corona hitting the country hard along with businesses, but Topeka like no other when it comes to places in Kansas that have been hit hard. Topeka has always had a high crime rate, but this time around it has been so ridiculously high that people don't even want to come to visit or even get on I-70 anymore to go through it. People have been moving out of Topeka as fast as possible and the best way that they can, but the people coming to Topeka are the people desperately leaving larger MidWest cities to Kansas. Lots of people from Detroit, Chicago, Indianapolis, Saint Louis, Des Moines, Omaha, etc. It is ridiculous how bad Topeka has become and here I am in this city to restore it and it's people from getting any worse. As Dani and I are in the heart of the downtown area being guided around by this older dub dub we are outside of this red brick school that looks like it has so much history to it as kids are inside playing although there are broken windows all around the place. I never even knew, thought of, or even heard of a school being in the downtown part of Topeka which amazed me from what I had just learned, but also depresses me from what I see. My mission is to get to the root of the problem that is stemming from the problem while I extend an olive branch to the people to help the city and other cities as well. So, my mission starts with Topeka, Kansas which I always thought would be Chicago first, but aye, this one hits closer to my hometown if you know what I mean. So as I take-note and create-hope for the great-folk here I go…………………………...*

Work Out Poyntz--- *So here I am today in the nice bright sunny day in my hometown of Manhattan, Kansas aka Wild City, Kanziss. I'm on Poyntz Avenue for a change of the scenery for my workouts right in front of a flower and bike shop across from a pizza shop all while being behind the Manhattan Mall. I have both my 40 pound dumbbells and my 45 pound dumbbells with me as I'm doing some sidewalk workouts such as sit ups and push ups. People are slowing down as they drive past me to record me and take pictures which I'm so used to that by now and I don't believe it's ever bothered me. People are slowly walking past me as I'm working out too. There was this old Black guy that walked by me that was acting weird and was looking at me from the corner of his eye as if he didn't trust me by him. I just let out a light laugh and continued on with my exercises. As a couple more people walked by in this sunny afternoon by me mainly old people or older people both Black and White that's when I decided I was going to try and get some videos and pictures of myself by setting my phone with magnets on this green pole so that I could get some flexing pictures with the mall right behind me and some of the red brick sidewalk behind me as well. I never used my photo timer on my phone before, but I'm gonna use it today so that I could get a different scenery and a different background for both my pictures and my videos to enhance the content and visuals, plus down on this side of town is a great setting. I placed my phone on the pole as I jog down the sidewalk so that I could get to my spot in time to take my pose and flex. After my picture was taken I saw this dub dub walking across the street not even on the crosswalk portion just walking across the street to reach the parking lot nearest to me which I could only imagine that she's going towards her vehicle. I'm thinking to myself "OUUU..she's a bad girl!" As she looks like she just got off of work as she's in a correction officers uniform. I pulled my phone from the green pole that it was on and I picked up my pace as I said "Aye! Excuse me. You wouldn't mind taking some videos and pictures of me would you?" That's when she smiled and said "No problem!" As she's pulling her phone out of her pocket although I'm reaching my phone out to her and she grabs my phone with her other hand and says "Oh. OK." Which I laughed because she must have* *thought I looked good, because not only was she willing to take pictures and videos of me, but she was willing to do it on her phone which would have lead to us exchanging either phone numbers, emails, or social media for me to get the pics and videos from her, but I can still get those either way if I wanted to. So I then say to her as she's following me with my phone and her phone in her hands. I went near that green pole where I had placed my magnetic phone earlier and I bent over to spin my dumbbells over to show me the weight of them as I decided to pick up my 45s and to leave the 40s where they were and to cross the street to get close to the mall. I stand back up with the 45s and I look at the dub dub and I tell her "Asiago. Let's go across the street to get some videos and pictures over there please." And that's when she had nodded her head and said "OK." Then that's when I said "I'm sorry. I didn't even ask to see if you were busy or in the middle of doing something else." That's when she responded back with "No. You're OK. I just got off of work and I don't do much, but go home after work." That's when I replied back with "Asiago! I feel you. Well thank you for taking your time to do this for me." That's when she responded back with a "No problem. No problem at all. You're welcome." Then that's when we got to walking down the sidewalk to cross over the crosswalk past the stop sign as I'm pumping my 45 pound dumbbells, but not getting the full form follow through because my arms are exhausted and my body is sore. As that dub dub is following behind me I could clearly hear her say "Guys that don't even talk "Black" aren't Black." And that's when we made it to this first store on the mall property as I put my 45 pound dumbbells onto the sidewalk and I stood back up and I turned around to look at that dub dub and that's when I said "Wow! Is that the new motto now?" That's when she gave me this "Oh shit! Oh fuck!" face and she said "I don't know." Then that's when these 2 Black guys had come outside of the store and the older Black guy looked at that dub dub and I and he said "Hello. How are y'all doing?" That's when we responded with "Good." And he said "Good." too in return as he looked at the dub dub's hands as she had a cell phone out in each hand. Then the younger Black guy which could have been his son was taking stuff back inside of the store which it has been so long since I could last remember a fully functional and operating store in this spot. The younger Black guy comes out and looks at the dub dub and I and he says "Hi." To us and wipes his hands off before putting it out there for the both of us to shake his hand. As we introduced ourselves that's when I said my name and he laughed and that's when he said "I knew you looked familiar, just a lot bigger. I remember when you would sell your CDs around town." When he made that specific chuckle that's when I knew he thought my music was whack when he either bought my CD or heard it. You could tell that these guys thought that this dub dub and I were together as a couple in a relationship too. That's when the older Black guy then asks us "What are y'all up to today?" That's when I responded with "Just working out for now. I was hoping that we could get some pictures and videos right outside of your shop if there's..........." Then as I looked behind me that's when that younger Black guy had already taken in this huge painting of a saxophone player playing the saxophone into the shop that I really wanted to take a picture by or at least do a video in front of since it was very appealing. That's when the older Black guy had looked behind me to see his son inside the shop with that photo as he caught onto what it was that made me choose this spot. That's when that older Black guy had looked at me and the dub dub and said "Sure! No problem. Go ahead." As he turned around to go back into the shop I assumed to bring some more stuff outside that he would like to be seen in my videos and pictures. As he went back inside that's when I told that dub dub "We can take some pictures of me in this corner flexing until they come back out." That's when she looked at me as she followed behind me and put up both of her arms to not only use my phone for these pictures and videos, but her phone as well. As I got in the corner and positioned myself for a pose that's when…………………………………………...*

The Train With My Fool--- *So as I'm on a train with one of the fools I've known since middle school and became really good friends with in high school named Stache. We used to always do dumb shit in this fools truck, but it was so fun at that time too. We always talk about that stuff whenever we see each other because we had a fun childhood together. Here we are though years later as adults that don't have near as much of the kind of fun that we did as teenagers as now it's always something planned out, scheduled, and paid for. We have to abide by the rules now, but it's always the most that we make of it. As we are seated in the same row with an open seat between us on our way to California together and………………...*

T.K.O. (Teeth Knocked Out)--- *I'm watching this big UFC Title Match as these 2 White guys are battling it out swinging at one another's heads as if they are trying to knock them off one anothers necks. The crowd, the announcers, and even the people at home are reacting so brutally as these guys are definitely going to feel these hits tomorrow. I can only imagine who's going to have a concussion or brain bleed. You can just see and feel what this belt means to these 2 fighters as they are willing to die in this ring to become a champion. Both of these guys extremely tatted up at middle weight class hitting and taking hits as if they are super heavyweights or something. I guess to give the crowd a show and to stick to their word they decided to make this a standing boxing match as none of these guys tried to wrestle or throw any kicks. "Hit for hit! So many hits that an album had just gone diamond and certified by the RIAA. So many hits in the ring that a domestic abuse call and a file for divorce was made. So many hits that the Pop Charts have these 2 guys tied for number one for the greatest songs. So many hits that these guys are now on The Rolling Stones magazine cover." I should definitely be a ringside announcer thinking about it as my verbal skills are on point and I'm so entertaining. As these guys still hit one another that's when one of the guys slips on what we assume to be was sweat and in the process of trying to regain his balance and footing that's when he had put his hands down and for those spit quick seconds it left him exposed as the guy that never lost his footing had swung so much harder when he saw that quick split window of opportunity and the opposing fighter could see it, but could not react in time as all he could do was tense up his body and face as that fist hit him so fucking hard in the jaw that you could hear everyone gasp as the impact took out his mouthpiece and a majority of his top row of teeth, maybe 8 or so. Blood, sweat, and tears literally from both of these fighters in the ring as one fighter falls down slowly with his eyes rolled in the back of his head and the crowd is silent and even the announcers were silent as this knockout was brutal. A Teeth Knock Out Knock Out that could have hurt more than this fighter's teeth. As everything had gone slow-mo and the referee ran to the fighter that got knocked out along with paramedics as well that's when things were starting to look a lot worse than just a knockout. That's when the program was interrupted by a commercial and…………………………...*

The Chingy Concert & My Kids--- *I'm on stage at the D.C. (Douglass Center) in my hometown of Manhattan, Kansas aka Wild City, Kanziss on the SouthSide. Why? Because the rap artist Chingy is on stage performing for a small crowd of people seated on the basketball court of the D.C. as Chingy is performing on this small ass stage with not much room to move around on or get hype with as there are long wooden tables behind him and equipment to work out with as well. One of the fools I grew up with's little brother that we call "Dark Mahl" is on the stage to the far left by the steps if you are facing the stage and for some reason a lot of his stuff is on stage that would normally be in a room at someone's house. With the amount of things I'm seeing and moving around I got the impression that this fool was living on the basketball court and sleeping on the stage. As most of the people in the crowd including 4 of my kids are young I could only imagine them either not knowing much of Chingy's songs or any at all. No one is really moving or standing up from their chairs and Chingy isn't really putting on a good performance. I don't know if it's because he hasn't performed in so long or because he doesn't really care about my town since it's a small college town and he just wants to get paid or what? As I'm moving around the stage to make Chingy more comfortable and have more space which should have been cleaned up and ready for him before everyone had shown up. As I'm moving around, that's when I had seen one of Dark Mahl's jump ropes that I lifted up while looking at him as he was still on the corner of the stage. He shrugged his shoulders and that's when I had walked the jump rope over to the other side of the gym stage to a hook I had seen. As I walked across the stage to the hook to place the jump rope on, that's when the mic and music had cut out in the process of Chingy rapping. Chingy still has the mic in his hand and he's trying to rap as loud as he can, but it just sounds worse. That's when I could see my kids in the crowd, especially my daughter, who looked so disappointed and annoyed. Then that's when.......we ended up being at my last job at Ag Press as my MBO Folder was running and I was staring at it by the metal pillar that my extra sheets of paper would go on a skid as seeing the rollers pull my paper to the next unit..........Then, I end up outside somewhere on a sunny day in a grassy field with all 4 of my kids playing as if we had planned a picnic and my youngest son being so much taller and older looking that it blows my mind to see all of my kids here playing and having a good time......Then we end up in this house where my kids are in this small living room all older and taller as I look at them in an emotional state to see my creations here in front of me healthy, happy, and in my custody. My oldest son has his leg out as my youngest son is just tapping his leg to the point where you could hear the leg bone being tapped and my oldest son throws his head back and he says "Daddy help me! He's hurting me!" As all of my other kids laugh and I tell them "He's just having fun! I love y'all. What do y'all want to do today?" Then that's when my daughter says "Daddy!" With a big beautiful smile on her face and she says............................*

The Super Bowl Rematch--- *For the first time in sports or football history a championship game was challenged the day after the championship was declared and for the Super Bowl 2021. The Kansas City Chiefs versus The Tampa Bay Buccaneers was overruled to be replayed tonight. The day after the Buccaneers declared their Super Bowl victory and Tom Brady receiving his 7th championship ring the Chiefs have another chance of getting the win. For the first time ever this has been done. With all the flags thrown the night before and the tightest defense I have seen being played on the Chiefs the pressure was a lot for Mahomes* *and the Chiefs. The MidWest and Chiefs fans were left sour last night, but tonight some of that anger and resentment and revenge could and should be turned into fuel and passion to making double history tonight with 2 Super Bowls in one year as The Chiefs and The Buccaneers stand across the field from one another for the anthem and……………………………....*

A Trucker's Talk--- *I'm in this small house with this White family that I have no idea how I met or got here, but they are being pretty cool and not making me feel awkward, uncomfortable, or unwanted here…..For right now. It's 2 young White kids, one teenage girl and one teenage boy. The mom is this overweight dub dub with long thin hair that you could tell lounges around the house all day from the position she sits in on the couch and the thin light colored nightgown she wears at home. The husband is this redhead White guy that gives off the impression that he use to or that he has a lot of Black friends. Him being a trucker he's giving us these trucker stories and the things he's seen on the road and the places he has been to. Throughout him talking about his road stories that's when he had remembered that he had someone that was interested in the thick tire mountain bike that he or no one in his household used so he wanted to get it out of the house, but was kind of hesitant because the roads were really bad with the snow and the ice. He knew the roads were bad, but he kept talking about how he wanted the bike out of the house and how bad he wanted to help people out. The weather being the only obstacle or thing making him fight his emotions right now as he stopped talking for a few moments and we all looked around the room and at him with that "OK. What should we do then?" look on our faces. It was getting late, like almost 10p.m. late and this fool is talking about getting on the roads in his truck to drive from this small SouthWestern town here in Kansas to Wichita, Kansas which is a little over an hour there then stay for I don't know how long because this fool is being so emotional right now and is talking so much. It's already past my bedtime so I know I'm going to fall asleep in this truck. I figured he would want me to go because he doesn't know me that well to leave me in his home especially with his wife or even his kids because if it was the other way around I know that I wouldn't leave my family in such an uncomfortable position like that either. Then that's when that guy yelled out "Ah Ha! I got it figured out! All of y'all get your stuff ready now! We're taking a ride to drop this bike off now. Everybody bring what you want to bring on the road and let's get out of this house, take a trip, and have some fun"………So here we are now, on this icy ass and snowy road taking a turn off of the road ramp onto the highway as the dad looks so uncomfortable as if he knows this was a bad idea as we are all up front with him. I don't think I feel uncomfortable about this drive, but I'm giving this fool the benefit of the doubt. I'm so tired and I want to sleep, but at the same time I'm so uncomfortable I'm not completely sure how this is gonna go so I'm staying awake the best that I can as we are riding in this slow moving truck with a flat tire bike in the trailer of the semi as the weather conditions get worse as the seconds go by and that's when…………………..*

Stripper In Our House--- *So it's early morning and I'm at my desk writing out the dreams I had when I was asleep. My maintain and I had the house to ourselves as the boys had stayed the night at their grandparents. My maintain had gotten up about 10 minutes after me which is really weird because she doesn't like to wake up early at all. As I'm writing I could hear movement on the couch beside me which I assumed was my son until I had remembered that* *both of the boys were staying at their grandparents. I turned around to see this grown ass woman get up from the couch while she's in heels with a thong on and just a towel that she opens wide just to close the towel tight and to cover up her bare, but nice looking titties because she doesn't have a bra on for some reason. My maintain is in the laundry room as this tall ass very light skinned mixed feezy walks towards the kitchen as her heels clink and clunk on our trailer floor and she walks into the kitchen directly across from my right shoulder of mines and she reaches over the counter to the fruit bowl not even 2 feet from me, but in that process she had dropped her towel which I'm going to assume was purposely. That's when I looked over at her to see her titties out and this nice beige thong as we made eye contact and she gave me this look of her wanting to fuck me until my maintain had peaked from around the corner from the laundry room and said "Na uh! What did I tell you girl?! I told you that you need to have your clothes on at all times if I'm going to let you stay at my house!" That's when I had went back into writing and that feezy had an "Oh fuck!" face on as she slowly reaches down to pull the towel back over her with a green apple in her hand and she turns around slowly then tells my maintain "Sorry! I'm so tired and the towel fell down when I went to reach for an apple".................................*

Turning Off The Light--- *So I'm in my trailer about to go to sleep with my maintain. Right before my maintain and I go to sleep though I got up from the bed to go into the kitchen and the living room to turn off the lights. As I walked through the kitchen to turn on the light above the stove I saw a White girl's arm move up above the couch and I hear heavy breathing and moaning on where my 3 year old son was supposed to be sleeping. I stepped out of the kitchen slowly and towards the living room and guess what the fuck I saw?! 2 White people, guy and girl fucking on MY living room couch! "What the fuck?!" I yelled out as they both lifted their heads up over the couch to look at me and the guy which is on top of the dub dub looks and gives me the head nod and says "What's up dude?" And the dub dub waves while a dick is inside of her and she says "Oh. Hi!" That's when I said "What the fuck?!" And I turned around to go back into the room to ask my maintain if she invited these people into our fucking home and if she knew they were fucking on our couch? As I turned around those people on the couch went right back to fucking as I could hear the couch erk and jerk and both of them breathing heavily until I reached the room to ask my maintain….That's when the room light was on bright as fuhh and it was one of the boxing trainers I had back when I had taken boxing classes named Jock Nitchell in bed with HIS girlfriend I assume as the bedroom is layed out so different as there's a closet to the left of me and I know that somehow I am no longer in my home and that's when Jock Nitchell looks at me and he tells his maintain about how he needs to sell his drums and…………………………..*

The War At Home--- *There is a huge war with America and some countries in the Middle East that even stretches to parts of Russia. Threats of a missile attack have been called on both sides and troops have already been shipped and flown off to Army bases nearest to the enemy's soil. This war has had people more paranoid and in panic and fear than the whole 2020 Corona pandemic. We need our men and women focused as we don't know how long this war will last and how deadly it could get. As a lot of the troops have been sent off to fight there are still some units and platoons that are training and getting ready to fight. What's been* *holding back most units though is domestic problems. This is what most Army people call "Domestic Terrorism" as "The War At Home" between Army spouses has been a historical all time high and many Army members are ending up more fucked up with PTSD, suicides, and domestic abuse than ever before. These military members are losing focus before they even go to their Army bases or before they even put on their uniform. The calls have been so ridiculous, as my cousin's husband has even been a victim of this as she's been fighting with her husband on the daily and she honestly doesn't even know why. That has been the answer for most spouses as they don't know what's been going on as if there has been a major chemical imbalance or if this war has caused so much panic and fear into people that it's caused people to lose their minds and try to justify it through acting irrational, but the widespread of this issue is just too ironic. So many military members on the American side have been going AWOL, committing suicide, been checking into mental wards, filing for divorce, going to jail, etc. That a deep investigation has been put into place over a course of months that investigators have been coming up with information on the infiltration of Army doctors altering the hormones in Army wives, food and water supply being tampered with, and medication of Army men to be psychedelics and hormone altering as well. Within interrogation some of these doctors, healthcare providers, store workers, and cops that are working for the people we are going to war against have admitted this method has been put into effect almost a year before the war was declared and that America WILL lose this war and lose so much money, power, and respect in turn. The war at home has been started with the war at home as there is so much infiltration and sophisticated methods that even with the information gathered many investigators don't know who to report to or how to report it in fear that there are so many other people working against the U.S. and…………………………………………………..*

Meeting Eminem--- *I'm walking into this building and upon walking into this building guess who the fuck I see seated behind this flimsy ass white foldable table? Yuh, you probably won't get it right unless you re-read the title of this dream. Yuh, that fool Eminem. By himself. Brown hair and beard and he's looking at me as I'm looking at him. "What the fuck?! You're big as fuck my dude!" Eminem says to me as I know this had to be him even more because of his voice too. I laughed and I said "Dizzamn! Eminem. This is frazy my daw. What are you doing here?" That's when he looked at me and said "I don't rap anymore so I hang out at clubs and bars scouting for new talent to recruit to my record label. Only the best of the best that can write a song, but be so lyrical to keep that real rap alive." That's when I said "Most def my daw that goes hard. Your love for rap is deeply a great passion." Then I thought about my music, but I didn't want to bring that up and ruin our energy. I will probably just bring that up later. For the little amount of silence between us as I'm standing on the other side of the white table and he's seated and I'm looking at his beard thinking of the famous "MGK" line when they were beefing and then I said "I bet Hailie was popular and yet so annoyed about everyone knowing that you were her dad." That's when Eminem looked at me and he cracked a smile, but right before he could answer that question that's when Eminem and I had somehow ended up in this big grassy field being chased by this wolf of some sort and…………………………………..*

Scooter Down The Hills--- *So my maintain and I are walking out of Flint Hills Place. We are leaving the entrance/exit by the stop sign by foot. As we are walking out past it that's when we* *see a group of Missionary dressed guys and girls on scooters, Razor scooters to be exact as they coast towards us. My maintain has already crossed the street towards the median as I watch from afar. I used to ride on Razor Scooters a lot back when I was a kid living in Flint Hills Place and here I am walking outside of Flint Hills Place with a whole bunch of White kids from a Missionary group on Razor Scooters. I was so impressed with so many memories popping up that I asked one of the Missionary scooter riding guys if I could ride their scooter. One of the girls was actually cool enough to let me do so as somehow my maintain was on a scooter next to me and we're going down the other hill to the right of this hill side by side which my maintain doesn't ride scooters or do anything like this at all or at least since I've been with her. I'm having so much fun on this scooter it's as if I don't want to give the scooter back. My maintain had to stop her scooter and give me that "What the fuck are you doing?" look to gain my attention. I stopped my scooter to look at my maintain as I said "What?!" and that's when she says "I think she wants her scooter back now." Then that's when I was calmed down to look around as all the Missionaries were looking at my maintain and I and the dub dub I had gotten my scooter from was looking at me smiling, but the guy that had let my maintain borrow his scooter was looking at us as if he was ready to fight us if we didn't give the scooters back…………………………….*

Rizza, Why?--- *So I'm in this trailer with this fat ass dub dub. Like she's the typical trailer trash fat White woman that only wears dresses because nothing else fits her well. One of the people I like and listen to is Rizza, but for some reason this is the guy I was convinced to jump with this White woman as I'm holding him down as the dub dub puts her weight down on him and tries to suffocate him and punch him. This guy is so much stronger than he looks as he's pushing himself up even with this fat lady on him and myself holding him down. After he pushes all the way up and gets this fat lady off of his back that's when he stands up from the bed and brushes his suit off and says "How you doing brother?" to me as that fat lady ran off into the kitchen where Rizza had slowly walked through and that's when that fat lady was by the kitchen island and she bent over real quick to pick up a baseball bat to throw over Rizza and she pulled out a thicker baseball bat for herself as I caught the one she had thrown to me and we walked in towards Rizza and started brutally beating him with these bats. I don't know why or how I was convinced to do this with this woman that I don't even know, but during and after this beating this was already an attempted murder for no specific reason at all to me. "What has gotten into me? What happened to me?" As I see Rizza so badly beaten I am looking at him so remorseful and knowing that this is not me. "How did this woman convince me to do so? This guy is so impactful and inspiring and here I am taking away someone that I was even inspired by." As he slowly dies my heart drops not knowing what the fuck I should do now. I feel so fucked and………………………………………………*

If You're Not Happy, Leave!--- *So I'm guessing it's a couples night all at my in-laws trailer. We are all gathered around the living room stretching to the kitchen. My sister and her husband at the kitchen table as my in-laws are on the couch by the wall before the hallway and my maintain and I on the couch with our backs against the window and another couple to our left on the wall right before entering the kitchen. I don't know who that other couple is, but I'm going to assume it's a friend of my sisters and her husband or maybe a friend of the in-laws My sister* *starts the conversation off by saying "I'm tired of not being taken serious and being cheated on when I do so much for him. I get no respect at all. I'm not happy anymore, but for some reason I just want to work this out." That's when I began saying "If you're not happy then you have got to have the self respect to leave. The more you stay the more you are complicating your happiness and your life. If he has no respect for you and you blatantly know this especially after y'all had a kid then it's time to leave or it's been time. If someone cheated on me I would be completely done. The love and respect would be gone for me because it was already done from the other person when they did what they did!" Then as I began expressing myself more and more that's when my maintain had nudged me and I looked at her and I said "What?!" as she just gave me this look, but I was being so passionate while expressing myself that I had went back into talking before I got nudged again this time harder as I looked at my maintain again as she signaled me towards her parents and I guess her mom was getting offended with what I was saying because she had cheated on her husband, but all I can do is honestly express myself whether that offends people or not would you rather be more mad at me for telling the truth or for telling a lie? And then we had went onto talking about……………………………...*

<u>Throwing Stuff Out, Late To Work, and Van On Grass---</u> *So after a long night of throwing away so much stuff of my maintain and I's oldest son from his clothes, to small tables, and desks which I'm surprised we're not donating, but we bagged them up and took everything else out to the curb. I'm waking up now to see that I'm late for work. "Fuck!" As I hurry up to gather as much shit that I need for work I head out the door without drinking my morning water or even eating any breakfast and I hopped in my maintains van for some reason not even thinking about her going to work or only seeing my monster in law in a house that I'm not familiar with. As I hopped in the van and rushed out of this driveway I ended up going down some neighborhood on the NorthView side of my hometown of Manhattan, Kansas aka Wild City, Kanziss. As I drive past this baseball field and what not I realized that I forgot something in that house I was just in and that I'm also headed the long way to work so with my anxiety rushing and not wanting to drive down this whole block that's when I just cut onto the grassy field before the baseball field and drove on it heading back towards that house and I could feel how wet the grass was from the vans tires and I……………………………………………………*

<u>Nutrition Store---</u> *So I'm inside of this nutrition store that I go in every so often to get on the scale for more in depth body composition testing. This scale levels out your muscle, bone, water, and dry weight and tells you your fat percentage. I come in here about 6 months to a year mainly becauseI hate these fools trying to sell me and tell me how supplements can and will only get me what I need bodybuilding wise plus these are the same fools that allowed me to sell my shirts in their shop then about a month later or less they told me to pick my shirts up which I'm pretty sure it was because I don't take supplements and I don't buy from them on the regular and it's so funny how the main guy doesn't believe that I'm all natural, but he fails to realize the kinds of workouts I perform, how long I've been doing these workouts daily and throughout the years, and how serious I am about what it is that I do. I step on the scale after taking my shirt and socks off being only dressed in my boxers and shorts as the scale can give a more accurate testing with the less amount of clothing that I have on. Now the owner of this* *shop loves to talk and he's always trying to sell me something that I really have no interest in. I just like their high tech scale. So as I'm on this scale and pressing in my info and then told to stand still he tells me a few moments later to step off of the scale as the computer calculates my body percentages. As I stepped off that's when the store manager steps from behind his desk and cash register and points out his shirts and supplements then he remembered right quick about me not believing in supplements then points at the jerky sticks in a green and gold wrapper. That's when he threw one to me and said "Here, try this out." As I caught it and looked at it then read the ingredients and saw that "pork" was one of the ingredients and that's when I said "Ah, you know I stopped eating pork almost a year ago? I'mma get some of those turkey jerky sticks I got last time." That's when the store manager looked at me and said "No. I didn't know that . How could I know that if you never told me that bud?" That's when I looked at him as he gave me a dumb sarcastic face and I looked at him with that "You make a good point." I looked around for the turkey jerky as I saw them wrapped in forest green plastic. I took them to the counter that he had hurried up and rushed behind for the scale, that was until I saw a few people walk into the store that I know. Big Dick Baddy and a few other ex coworkers came into the store. They all look at me in surprise and shock as Big Dick Baddy says out loud "Bryan! In a supplement store!" As I was such in shock from seeing them that I forgot about being at the counter so I went towards them as they sat at this round black table and we began talking and…………………………………………...*

ATV Visit--- *So after my daw ATV has been out of the Army for years and moved back to New York we have been linking up through social media about motivation and positivity and videos and seminars. He had decided to come back to Manhattan, Kansas for us to link up after years of not seeing one another and to talk more one on one about business. For some reason we are in this wooden clubhouse looking home or business on Fort Riley Boulevard across the street from my old job, Ag Press where this cheap tire place used to be. As ATV had just got done talking about business moves and what we had planned it was about 4:00 o'clock p.m. as I checked my phone and I stood up and I said "Asiago my daw. I'mma get ready to leave though. We can meet up tomorrow." As soon as I said that that's when I knew something was wrong. He gave off this look and I asked him "What's wrong?" That's when he responded back with "You said if I was to come out here you would clear your week for us to talk about business." That's when I looked out the window of this club house out to Fort Riley Boulevard watching cars drive by and some people walk across the street on that sidewalk and I thought about my workouts and my time with my family as my anxiety began to rush, but I had to calm it down because he did come all the way out here from New York to talk business as he did keep his word. As I turned around to tell him "You're right. I did say that." That's when I had seen my other fool from New York seated on a chair across from ATV who was seated in a chair across from him as they stared one another down. I looked at Starney and said "Starney? Dizzamn! What are you doing out here my daw? What are the chances that I see both of my daws from New York out here?" Then that's when my daw ATV had stood up from his chair and walked towards the window to look out of it and I told Starney "Y'all know y'all are both from New York right? He's from Brooklyn. Isn't that the borough you're from too?" Starney wouldn't even look at me or acknowledge me as he was just staring at ATV although ATV was looking out the window with his back facing him. That's when I caught on that these 2 fools didn't like* *one another, but I was confused to who followed who out here? What their problem was? And what was about to happen?...*

<u>Travis Scott In Manhattan---</u> *So my maintain and I are on Tuttle Creek Boulevard in my white Chevy Impala headed home. As I'm driving I don't know how or why, but I'm having thoughts of my daughter as she's imagining Travis Scott having a home in Manhattan, Kansas aka Wild City, Kanziss. This fool has a home on the top floor of some big tall loft or something and he's showing us around. As these thoughts are going through my head I'm still driving, but decided to turn around to go the other direction for some weird ass reason. Physically I'm driving, but mentally Travis Scott is walking us through his home. As I'm still driving past the rocky hills on the side of the boulevard and I pass Vista Burger and more of the rocky hills then I pass the stop light and I come close to where these 2 old hotels use to be that's when I subconsciously knew why my body had drove me to this place while I was mentally being walked through Travis Scott's loft. These hotels are sitting exactly where I would put my house. The hotel in the back is where I told my maintain I would like a home built or to turn that hotel into a house. As we drove past it and I'm thinking of how my house would look and everything around it that's when a cop comes zooming through on the street and flying through the parking lot as my maintain and I look at him like "What the fuck?!" As we follow behind him and in my head that's when Travis Scott mentions how he has 2 more homes here in Manhattan, Kansas and that's when he walks us out the door. Weird right?...*

<u>That Ass Whoopin'---</u> *So for some fuckin' reason I'm with my manager Ginger Snap as we are walking up the sidewalk to this nice looking and decent sized house. I don't know why I'm with Ginger Snap, but we're good and getting along. As Ginger Snap knocked on the door to whoever's house this was I'm just standing back waiting for the door to open and to see who and why we are here. After looking at the door and everything around us for about 20 or so seconds that's when the front door finally opens and it's some dub dub I have never seen before. She says "Hi!" to Ginger Snap and I and then she tells us to come inside so we stepped from the porch to inside this home as we looked around and saw some nice things inside that's when Ginger Snap and that dub dub were talking up for a little bit until this tall Black guy who I assume to be this dub dubs boyfriend or husband came out and he said "Hi." to Ginger Snap in a friendly way, but then as he looked at me we had locked eyes and noticed one another. This fake ass fool we call Shady Slime that tries to get with everyone's girl, but claims he's so real and has done some grimey things to his own friends behind their backs. I don't fuck with this fool at all and he knows he's done some grimey two faced shit. Now I know where this fool lives and I'm in his home and there was no faking the tension this fool and I had towards one another. The house is quiet as him and I stare one another down and the two feezies in here with us are extremely quiet as they look at the both of us. The tension was so tight that the feezies could feel it too and they were worried about what was the problem and why we didn't like one another. As soon as he had moved his right arm to do I don't know what, but I didn't want to take that chance I just started swinging on this fool hitting him as hard as I could as we moved from the front room to the kitchen and we're making noises as the 2 feezies are behind yelling and screaming. I was swinging on this fool as hard as I could as he was feeling the impact, but this fool could take a hit. I could hear his maintain screaming and yelling out about* *how she was going to call the cops and although we were in their house I didn't give a fuck because I told myself that the next time I saw this fool I wasn't going to play with him. We went from the kitchen to the garage as I'm still beating the shit out of this fool. I'm surprised I haven't blacked out at all during this process. As I'm still hitting this fool for what seems to have been like 20 to 30 minutes that's when this fool finally drops to the ground. As he hit the hard cement garage floor I felt my body ease up as it wasn't so tense and in defense mode anymore, but I was shaking from my adrenaline. I'm breathing heavy as fuck feeling as if I had ran 10 miles straight or something and feeling as if I'm about to have a heart attack. As I don't see the feezies anymore that's when I had walked past Shady Slime as he laid knocked down on the garage floor as I stepped into the kitchen to see both feezies in the living room then a loud ass knock on the front door already knowing that that was a cop knock as Shady Slime's maintain ran towards the door that's when Ginger Snap had ran towards me as the cops stepped foot in the house, 3 of them that's when Shady Slime's maintain was talking loud and fast while pointing at me about how I had attacked her boyfriend and how I had beat the shit out of him from the living room, through the kitchen and to the garage knocking him out and now she's screaming. Two of the cops walk towards me with their hands on their sides right over their hand cuffs and that's when Ginger Snap starts screaming while she gets in front of me blocking the cops and she's defending me while screaming "Don't do anything to him! He's good! Leave him alone! Don't arrest him! Please don't!" As the cops had slowed down and stopped to look at one another then back to the cop that was next to Shady Slime's girlfriend then back to Ginger Snap and I and that's when………………………..*

Suspicious Van Cops (Bad Cop Bad Cop)--- *Here I am with my daw J-Crook, one of my ex's "C", and some Black guy that is a DJ from J.C., the city we are actually in right now. We are in the back of this big big trailer attachment of some sort that has a bunch of expensive DJ and club equipment including a disco ball. You can tell that this fool put a lot of money into his craft along with earning a lot and it's definitely unique. We are taking the back road of J.C. for some reason that is by the police department, the JDC, the DMV, and some old ass bar that lots of the older crowd goes to. I am looking around while this DJ is either having someone drive his equipment or has the money for an expensive self driving car he is looking around admiring how we are admiring all of his equipment. This fool could literally throw a small party back here if he wanted to or he probably already has. As we go down this road more and more that's when the DJ steps down from his stage platform, but then the vehicle stops. We look around like "What the fuck?!" But the DJ is acting all calm and whatnot as if there shouldn't be a reason at all for stopping for anything bad. He walks down past us and goes to the trailer door and unlocks it from the inside then pulls it up and we are on that back road just a lot further down and the sun is out very bright. The DJ steps off of the trailer to his right and says "Whoa! Y'all need some help?!" That's when J-Crook, C, and I went to the end of the trailer to see what the fuck he was talking about and we saw this red car pulled over on the side of it being 1 guy and 1 girl with another Hispanic guy inside looking serious as fuhh as we all stepped off of the trailer with intentions of helping them. The guy and the girl on the outside of the red car were in great shape. The fit Hispanic guy had on a shirt, a white shirt that had boxing gloves on them with some red sweatpants. The Hispanic feezy had on a small tight white shirt with some nice ass black yogas on that made her ass pop out like "BLLLOOOOWWWWWWW!!" I'm assuming that* *the fit guy and the fit feezy were a couple. The not so in shape pissed off Hispanic guy in the red car had on a baggy off white shirt with a picture of boxing gloves on them and some red sweatpants as well. I'm assuming they were a part of a boxing team. We all had intentions of helping them, that was until we heard cop sirens behind us as we all looked in the direction of them as they pulled up slowly towards us. Now me being from Manhattan, Kansas I always thought that J.C. had a weird police station because all of their cops were K9 units in SUV's. Which that alone always told us that J.C. had a major drug problem. What was pulling up on us though was no SUV though, it was a big transportation van with sliding doors and tall enough to hold luggage above the heads and it was a glossy black and white painted color. We all looked at them like "Good. They could help get this car off the road and maybe a tow or some jumper cables. The van stops and these 2 White cops step out of the van and walk towards us and I don't know about everyone else, but I just got a bad vibe from these cops. They made me feel as if they weren't here to help us. As they stepped closer and closer to us I'm looking around at everyone trying to signal them, but everyone was focused on these cops. These 2 White cops that look like they abuse their power and don't like anyone that's not White walking up to us with these smirks on their faces with 3 Black guys, 2 Hispanic guys, 1 Hispanic feezy, and 1 dub dub. 7 of us and 6 of us are undesirable to these 2 White cops that are smirking the closer and closer they get the more and more of bad vibes I'm getting from them. They stop a couple of feet from all of us and the cop that was in his drivers seat when they pulled up says "What's the problem here?" That's when the DJ and one of the Hispanic guys started to explain at the same time, but the cop that was the passenger yells out "YOU'RE BLOCKING THE FUCKING ROADWAY WITH ALL OF THIS STUPID BLINGY DJ SHIT FROM ONCOMING TRAFFIC AND THIS PIECE OF SHIT RED CAR IS GOING TO GET FUCKING TOWED!" That's when I yelled out "First off this is a backroad with not much traffic and we pulled over to help these people out and if not we were headed back to our destination. Plus with the size of this trailer it's not like we could have pulled over on the side without tipping over." That's when everyone besides the cops started nodding their heads in agreement. Both of those cops had stepped in closer towards us and started yelling at us "GET IN THE BACK OF THE FUCKING VAN NOW! NOW!!!!! WE'RE GOING TO SEARCH BOTH VEHICLES WHILE WE TAKE Y'ALL DOWN TO THE STATION!" We all looked around at the cops then at one another like "What the fuck?!" That's when C yells out "YOU CAN'T DO THAT!" That's when the passenger cop yelled out "SHUT UP BITCH! STICK TO YOUR OWN KIND DIRTY PUSSY ROTTEN BITCH!" Then that Hispanic feezy with her thick accent yelled out "DON'T TALK TO HER…" before she could even finish her sentence that's when those 2 White cops had pulled out their guns towards us and said "Get in the back of the fucking van now!" That's when the fit Hispanic guy stepped up and said "Y'ALL CAN'T FUCKIN'...." and before he could even finish his sentence that's when both of the cops said "FUCKIN' TEST US!!!" I noticed how these cops got even more pissed whenever someone that wasn't White would talk back to them. Then that's when the cops said "We don't have enough cuffs to arrest all of y'all and we're doing this the nice way. Do y'all want us to get back up and have this end up being deadlier than it could and should be?" That's when they had waved their guns to the van as all 7 of us lined up to walk towards the van as the passenger cop opened the sliding door. Weirdly enough the inside of this van was nice. The seats weren't plastic like you normally see in the back of cop cars; they had the original cushion seats and all, but there was a plexiglass barrier dividing the front two seats from the back passengers. We all sat where we could as the 2 cops buckled up and sped off down the road leaving both parties vehicles and yet neither one of those cops had radio'd anything in. My suspicions are rising and my adrenaline is rushing, but I have to control myself to think myself out of this situation effectively. As the cops sped off for about a couple of blocks or 3 we ended up on this familiar road which was one of the busy roads in J.C. The cops parked a block away from Church's Chicken restaurant and they unbuckled their seat belts while looking back at us and they said "Y'all better sit tight! We will be right back!" That's when we had all nodded in agreement because there really wasn't much else we could do. Then before they had stepped out of this transportation van the driver cop said "I'mma need y'all to buckle up before we get out of this van though." As he watched us and everyone had reached for their seat belts and clicked them in, that's when I had mines, but I put it close to my buckle, but didn't click it in. My daw J-Crook was seated next to me and I could tell from his body language and positioning of his feet that he was going to get the fuck out of the van with any moment of opportunity he had. The cops had stepped out of the van and walked towards Church's Chicken and that's when I had looked around at everyone and I said "I don't know about y'all, but these cops are suspicious as fuck to me. I feel like they're either going to set us up or kill us." That's when the people that I was with agreed, but the Hispanics looked at me as if I was frazy. I looked over at my daw J-Crook and he had the sliding door cracked open and he said "I'm getting the fuck out of here!" I looked around at everyone else as I let my seat belt go and I asked "Are y'all seat belts able to unbuckle?" Everyone reached for their seat belts and I heard a lot of unbuckling. "I find it weird how aggressive these fools are and how no calls have been reported or called in. I don't like these fools. Let's get the fuck out of this van and the fuck out of this city. We're gonna go back to our vehicles and try to get y'all red car to work. If not come on the DJ Machine aka The Club On Wheels with us and we're gonna head straight to I-70 and get the fuck far away from jurisdiction so they can't fuck with us." Everyone agreed as we had sat up from our seats and my daw J-Crook had slid open the transportation van door and we all jumped out of the van and ran down the block. As we ran towards the back road where we had our vehicles placed, that's when the chubby Hispanic guy kept bumping into me and trying to trip me as we were running. I sped up and this fool was still trying to do the same thing so I stopped where I was at and he stopped with me and I asked him "What the fuck is your problem my daw? I'm on your side trying to help us all." That's when he had pushed me so I swung on him and hit him as hard as I could knocking him down to the ground and kicking him and punching him until his body had went stiff and I had kept punching him in the face until I got up and looked where everyone else had ran and I ran to catch up to them. I couldn't believe that that fool had acted like that. As I ran the rest of the way towards where our vehicles were left that's when I had seen some people outside of both of the vehicles acting weird as the people I was with were pushing that crowd away and then…………………………...*

The Chicken At Ross--- *Here I am stepping into the Ross store in my hometown of Manhattan, Kansas aka Wild City, Kanziss. This is my maintain's favorite store plus they do have good clothes, books, and prices here. As I stepped in I instantly noticed these hoodies hanging up that go so hard! I have never seen any K-State hoodies that looked this nice with so much design on them. The printing on them was creative with the WildCat symbols and things around the hoodie that represented everything about K-State and Kansas in general. I wanted* this hoodie so bad. On one side of this rack the price said $7, but where these K-State hoodies were it had a price listed of $91. I said "What the fuck?!" outloud. "My discount would still be a lot to pay for these. Fuck!" As bad as I wanted these nice ass hoodies I just couldn't allow myself to spend close to $100 for a hoodie right now. I put the hoodie back on the rack and walked away hoping to come across something else that would take my mind off of the hoodies. As I walked about 3 racks down that's when I heard a chicken sound that I assumed was someone listening to something or watching something with chickens with the volume really loud or someone playing with a toy until I saw……...A FUCKING CHICKEN step out and right in front of me clucking and walking. I'm looking down and then around to see if anyone else is seeing what the fuck I'm seeing, but naw I'm the only one. "What in the fuhh is going on here? This is frazy as fuhh!!" As I stared at this chicken I reached for my cell phone in my pocket and I instantly went for my SnapThat app. I unlocked my phone and opened the app and began recording this chicken as it walked throughout the store and I'm following it and this chicken is acting as if he can juke me away, but I'm still following behind this chicken. As I approached 30 seconds of recording this chicken and looking at this chicken from my phone then lifting my head over the phone to watch the chicken too that's when this chicken had dropped to the ground and had it's head to the side and it's wings somewhat open and this chicken was literally playing dead. I got all excited and started laughing because I have never seen or heard of a chicken playing dead before or even knew this existed up until now and here I am with this being recorded. "What the fuhh?! Wing stop! This chicken is actually playing dead right now! This is frazy!" I say out loud as my SnapThat is approaching the 60 second mark that's when I was so hyped up to save this video to my phone and to upload it whenever and wherever I could and as my phone was saving it and I was about ready to put it on "My Story" on SnapThat that's when…………………………...

The Work Argument (Anger Management)--- Here I am, at my "favorite fuckin' place" to be for over 8 hours of my day doing what I don't really give a fuhh about, along with everyone else here, but we have to in order to pay our bills and do some of the things we have to work hard and spend more time at this job to travel, buy things, order things, etc. Yuh, I'm at work! I'm already hearing my annoying ass managers voice right outside of my screen print machine talking about how I didn't sanitize my hands. I'm already or I have already been so fed up with this job and where I am with my life that I'm just agitated and so easily annoyed now. No one has masks on as the pandemic dumb shit has been over with for a few months now. I look at my manager and I tell her "Do you only pay attention to me? Because I know for a fact that I'm not the only one that doesn't use this hand sanitizer all the time, but you always talk to me about any and everything it's starting to get fucking annoying." As soon as she had heard me cuss that's when she had stepped back as her eyes had gotten all big. Then that's when this blonde dub dub had said something to the manager about a shirt and my manager had directed her attention to the question being asked which I thought was pretty weird and rude because she had just butted in and that's when I had said "That's rude!" To the both of them and my manager had looked at me and she said "No it's not." That's when I said "Are you fucking serious rght now? She just rudely interrupted us when she had seen us in a conversation and that's not rude? Then then what the fuck is rude?" That's when my manager had turned back to the blonde dub dub and I said to my manager "Meet me in your office. Now!" As I walked *right towards her office not even looking to see if she was following behind me as I sat in the computer chair behind hers and as I sat down I saw her walking into the office looking timid as she shut the door behind her. I noticed how this office was expanded to where there were also more windows where there used to be a wall too. As my manager had sat down, that's when my manager says "Look, I know you have to be a little frustrated with your ex C being charged for all of those drugs, but you have got to…" That's when I had cut her off and said "I know nothing about my ex catching drug charges and that's not even why I'm frustrated." Then that's when my young country coworker came out of nowhere and said "Yeah. They're charging her with all but one of the multiple drug charges. She's looking at a lot of time." Then that's when my manager had nodded her head and stood up and walked away with my country coworker as I stood up and that's when that blonde dub dub that rudely interrupted my manager and I earlier had stepped into the office next to me and stopped like a little over a foot from me and pointed at my dick and asked if she could borrow my pen. That's when she kept her finger pointed at my dick as she smiled and I reached in my pocket for my wallet and my pen and as I was handing my pen to her that's when……………...*

Mac Dre DVD--- *It's as if I'm on set as the filming of the Mac Dre DVD's are going on. Mac Dre has been putting out music back to back and it's going to show the world why he is deserving to be known for his movement and his style. Not only has his DVD's been about the recording process and the independent music hustle, but it has also been with entertainment such as mini series and episodes that are funny. One particular episode Mac Dre is in a diner that resembles the diner from The Wayans Brothers TV show and there's some White guy that comes up to Mac Dre which I'm going to assume is his agent and they're talking about business moves and a commercial for a chicken restaurant. Mac Dre looks at his agent and says "Tell that chicken place that I wants to be gettin' me chicken for the chicken yadadamean?" Then the audience starts laughing. Then Mac Dre's agent says "Come on Dre! This is an opportunity to get paid, have another sponsor, and for your face to be seen by a broader audience!" Then Mac Dre responds with "The Mac already has an audience of broads, but I guess I can do my thing dizzle for me paper." Then that's when Mac Dre's agent says "Good! Good! I will make the phone call and let them know that it's a go!" Then the agent guy walks off while he's digging in his pocket for his cell phone. As Mac Dre sits down to get ready to eat, that's when I'm looking at Mac Dre thinking about the impact this man has left before his passing the first time and how he was so blessed to get a second chance at life and how he is a humble hustler. The moves he's making now with the work ethic even stronger. The things he's accomplishing with a tighter circle and the people he has helped out along the way. I'm actually inspired with this man's work ethic and his entertainment that extends far beyond music alone. With his mini series, his dance DVDs, his music, his tour and live performances, etc. Mac Dre is and probably still will remain an independent rap artist, but I'm sure he will reach the mainstream status with his hustle and hardwork………………………………………………………...*

Joyner Lucas TV Show--- *Now when it comes to rap artists of today you cannot forget to mention the creativeness of Joyner Lucas. This man's music and features along with remixes and his creative videos are definitely a one of a kind. This man has even been pushing out an app that he had a part in creating for musician's whether that be underground or mainstream* *that saves artists and producers so much time and money in the creation of their craft and music. Now with this TV show Joyner Lucas is the narrator and he brings up instances from the early season of him being a little boy. The traumatic experiences that play a major role in his personality and upbringing. Joyner is having a flashback of a brown bear chasing his mom and him through this place that looks deserted as his mom and him are running together towards this road where there are some cars driving by. This bear is pissed off and vicious and is ready to kill. Joyner is screaming for his dad to come rescue and save them as his mom is running as fast as she can to get the both of them to safety. As they run and jump off the side hill towards oncoming traffic there is this SUV type burgundy vehicle that sees Joyner and his mom so she stops the vehicle and unlocks her doors for the two of them to get in. As Joyner is thrown into the back seat by his mom as she screams at the bear before she jumps in the backseat with young Joyner that's when the bear jumps onto the back of the SUV as everyone inside of the vehicle is screaming for their lives. This bear is huge! Huge enough to bear hug the SUV and have it's head right over the sunroof of this vehicle. As the driver is trying to peel off the bear is clinching both sides of the vehicle as tight as it could and digging its claws into the side of the vehicle more and more that the driver is desperately trying to peel off. Then that's when it showed Joyner Lucas as a little boy still walking into a dark room into his mom's house slowly and it was as if that whole scene was inside of the mind of Joyner Lucas as a little boy with a big imagination. The fact that he had yelled for his dad to come rescue him and his mom had touched me because whenever I was going through my roughest of times growing up I had always wished and hoped that my dad would come to rescue me so I wouldn't be so alone and figuring it out the hard way, but now that I'm older I can't complain much about my upbringing because it has taught me some valuable lessons and experiences that make me smarter and wiser beyond belief. As young Joyner is being shown on the TV screen that's when.................*

Kali Muscle In McDonald's Drive Thru--- *So here I am in the passenger's seat of Kali Muscles black Escalade. Now usually his videographer would be the one recording in the passenger's scat seat, but I guess I'm that guy now. The line is long and piled up. Frazy thing about all of this is how we are in my hometown of Manhattan, Kansas aka Wild City, Kanziss during the process of all of this instead of Los Angeles. The 4th Street McDonald's. As we are in this long ass line and cars and trucks are all behind us and in front of us that's when Kali Muscle begins spazzing out about how he needed his McDonald's right now and he started convulsing as if he was about to have a seizure. As I'm recording all of this and laughing that's when Kali Muscle then says "I'm going inside to get my fucking McDonald's right now! Fuck this! I'm hungry than a motherfucker!" Then that's when he points in the driver's seat as he steps out of his Escalade and slams the door and does his funny walk as he's headed into the McDonald's restaurant. That's when I sat my camera on the dash and got into the driver's seat as the line was slowly beginning to move. This Escalade was wide as fuhh and stood tall. My short ass had to lean up while adjusting the seats and that's when...........................*

Lost Your Van--- *I'm driving my maintain's van in this cold ass weather coming up the hill that is Tuttle Creek Boulevard after leaving Fort Riley Boulevard. It's snowy as fuhh outside and slick in certain places. As I'm getting closer and closer to the Short Stop gas station on the NorthView side of town, that's when I hit that first stop light and I take a right to go down the hill* *before taking a quick left which that small stop sign has a lot of snow on the road. Now I'm thinking I should either go around or just speed up and slide through the snow. I decided right quickly that I might as well just go to my left through all of this snow since I'm already over here. As I take a quick left and I slide through the snow while mashing down on the gas pedal that's when the van starts sliding while slush is being thrown all over the place. For some dumb ass reason though I decided to jump out of the van while I landed on the snow as my maintain's van drove off towards a parked car waiting in line by the gas pump and towards the gas pumps. I must have gotten so hypnotized from so much Bay Area Ghost Riding The Whip that I just had the impulse to do so. Now that is the meaning of going stupid doo doo dumb. As I'm knocking the snow off of me and watching my maintain's van maneuver through the snow that's when I ran towards it hoping that it wouldn't run into another vehicle or pump, but somehow it turns by itself towards a parking spot over by SubWay, but then it goes right past it and down the hill. I continued to run towards it and I looked right over the hill which down below is a trailer park that I just assumed my maintain's van had plowed through one or a few of them. I see the tire tracks, but I don't see the van at all or any damage that the van should have caused, but I'm glad it didn't, but where the fuhh is our van? I'm looking over this hill thinking in my head "Fuck! How do I explain this to my maintain or anyone at that?! I know there are some cameras around the gas station and this small bank, but they're gonna ask me "Why did you jump out of the van?" Fuck! Fuck! Fuck!"..*

<u>Suicidal K-State Girl---</u> *I'm running on K-State Campus with some faculty members and some students because we had gotten a call that some feezy is talking about killing herself. We don't know where she is at specifically as we are just running through halls and buildings that most people go to and what places we are told she could be at. Maybe this is a distraction from something else to happen even bigger as The Campus Raper has still been free and out on the loose and has become more sophisticated and sly on his tactics due to the cameras and the call lights newly placed around campus. We are running through hall after hall to go through rooms and asking and recruiting people to help us find this girl that is supposedly going to harm herself so that we could help her out. Some of these doors we are kicking in we are startling students, some students are fucking whether it's guy and girl, girl on girl, or guy on guy. We're even running into people that are doing drugs, but none of this is our concern because we are desperately trying to find this feezy so that we could help her out and prevent her from hurting herself or others. As we go through more and more places there's a lot of people hitting on me, but I'm desperately telling them that we need to find this girl and if anyone has seen or heard anything. No one seems concerned or worried about this. This one tall White feezy pulls me to the side and slams me against the wall and starts rubbing up on me and making out with me and that's when the dorms and sorority houses had popped up in my head and then……………...*

<u>The Maintenance Man Cheating---</u> *So there's this maintenance man that I work with that is fixing more than the machines and pipes at our job. He's lubing his pipe and fucking like a machine when it comes to our feezy coworkers. This fool has been fucking a lot of the feezies here and everyone is curious to how and why he does it when he is married and most of these feezies are married or are in relationships as well. Where is he doing this at? Is it at work?*

Under or outside of the machines? Are there more employees that he's fucked or is fucking now that we don't know about? This maintenance man, is he good with his tools or is he just a good "tool?" Is he fixing the company but being a "homewrecker?" Should he be a porn star? Is he getting paid on the clock while they're on his cock? We don't know, but there's literally "tricks and trades" to being The Maintenance Man…………………..

<u>Missa's Mom's Movement---</u> *Here I am in Flint Hills Place at the apartment that our friends that were mixed with Korean and Black lived in. For some reason, I'm in the bathroom taking a piss inside of this apartment that I don't know who the fuck lives in at this moment while taking the piss, but seeing my maintains laptop on the edge of the tub already a little bit wet on the side. I'm still pissing while looking at it like "What the fuhh?!" Until I finished my piss, shook my dick, and flushed the toilet with my shoe. I reached out to grab the laptop and I accidentally knocked it in the tub where there was some water in it already. "Fuck!" I said out loud probably fucking up her laptop even more. I got to thinking as I picked it up though and shaking it off and opening it and I'm thinking "Why the fuck would my maintain's laptop be here and why in the bathroom on the tub that was wet inside? What the fuck is she doing?" As I stepped out of the bathroom and through the apartment to see no one in here at all in the kitchen or the living room, but I assumed everyone had gone outside. As the laptop is dripping on me and on the floor I reached the front door and opened it to go outside on this hot and sunny summer day I see the whole neighborhood outside with Missa's mom speaking loud as if she is about to start a protest. Everyone is gathered in front of her and being very attentive as she speaks loudly and I never knew that Missa's mom was this blonde lady that I have seen around town before. I've seen her before, but never thought this was her mom. I thought her mom was dead to be honest with you. She has a very powerful and convincing voice along with attitude as I don't know what they're talking about, but it's gained my attention as I almost forgot why I came outside with my maintain's laptop and that's when………………………..*

<u>Finances With An Actor---</u> *Here I am in my 1971 Chevy Caprice with one of the fools I met through GramInsta who is an actor and a man of his word. At first I thought this fool was just saying what he could simply because he was an actor with a lot of followers and recognition. In fact this fool has so many more followers than me and he's a legit actor from all of the things I've seen him post. He congratulates me on my motivation and positivity and I congratulate him for being in the acting business. The reason why I say that he's a man of his word is simply because once him and I began following one another on GramInsta he did say that once he would be done shooting his season specifically for me to start training him that he would come to Kansas to get some training. Guess what?! He is out here and after a session of personal training here we are sitting in my Caprice as my daw Double B aka Dubbby goes over strategies on how to make my money work and build to an accumulation that a 9 to 5 job couldn't do. I've been tired of working for the past 4 to 5 years and now I've been researching stocks and IRA's retirement funds, stocks, etc. for the past 3 or so months and I've been ready to get out of this rat race and not living check to check. In exchange for personal training my daw Dubby is showing me so much information on how to advance in life and to do and be better because I am so deserving. As we are going over more and more examples and actually downloading an app and what to invest in and also how much and when that's when………………………*

Missa & MY Maintain--- *I'm walking towards the southside gas station coming from the car wash that has frozen chunks of ice on the side of the wall that is a nice big block of ice and on the ground is a thick sheet of ice that has a little bit of running water underneath it. This winter has been one of the coldest winters in years in Kansas with temperatures reaching the low negatives of -20 and almost -30. People have been avoiding going outside and many people's pipes have been frozen and power outs and black outs across Kansas and power shut offs to reserve energy for Kansas City. These past 2 years have been so frazy! It's been so frazy that even Texas has been hit with a lot of snow and ice and these fools don't even know how to drive in that shit. So anyways as I'm leaving the car wash part and coming in by the gas station sidewalk that's when I walk past the big glass window and I see my maintain sitting on the inside bench with this cardboard in her hand with plastic over it as she's at the table with someone, some dub dub that I'm assuming was just some random feezy that was at the gas station that just so happened was friendly and sat across from my maintain on this bench as they're both waiting for someone to get them. As my maintain looks up and sees me through the glass and she smiles at me that's when I gave her a goofy smile back and then that dub dub looked at my maintain then through the glass at me and you could see the face of this dub dub go from "I'm having a good time." To "Oh shit! It's him!" You see, this dub dub has no reason at all to not like me, but I don't like her because of some ignorant and stereotypical things she has said to me when she has mixed Black and White kids of her own that she needs to set a better example for. I walked into the gas station as Missa and I glared at one another then she looked away as I paid my attention to my maintain being excited to see her. My maintain and Missa were both seated at the bench with this cardboard that had saran wrap around it that they had to pull back and use a green scrubber to scrub the cardboard to a greenish tint all over for some reason. I don't know if it was to sooth them or what, but that's what they were doing and the more I stood by my maintain while Missa was here the more my adrenaline and anxiety began to rush as I so badly wanted to confront Missa, but I didn't want to come off just yelling and going off so I started clenching my fists and breathing out and in heavily to try to reduce my anxiety and that's when…………………………...*

Gay Fray?--- *So here I am late at night in my Caprice in front of this house that my headlights are shining on. I was told to come to this specific house in this specific neighborhood to pick up someone for a good paying money mission. As my lights are shining at the front door that's when this short, but buff ass Black fool steps from out of the darkness shirtless right in the direction of my headlights just staring at me. I'm looking at this fool like "What the fuck is this fool doing?" And "Is this the person I'm supposed to be picking up?" As he stares me down and I'm looking at him that's when I recognized who this fool was. I actually went to school with this fool. It's the fool Gay Fray and as soon as I recognized who he was that's when I opened my car door to step out and……………………...*

Lil' Bow Wow Break Up--- *Over the years Lil' Bow Wow has been in the media for a lot of bad stuff and gossiping controversy. From him getting jumped backstage at a B.E.T. event, from him falling off stage while performing, to him supposedly being broke, and from that elevator altercation with his maintain that ended up with an assault and battery once they got off the* *elevator or something like that. Aye, I don't know this fool or the struggles he is dealing with internally or how fame and controversy affects him, but I can only imagine how he truly feels. Now with all of that being said Lil' Bow Wow is back in the media and this time it's for a new date, partner, girlfriend, or fiancee he has been involved with. Nothing out of the norm right? That was until we found out that he has been sexually involved and invested with a fucking hologram! Yuh, you heard that and read that right. Everyone says Lil' Bow Wow has lost his fucking mind! Literally and metaphorically speaking. As he's on this talk show seated right next to this hologram as his arm goes through her and she's flashing in and out at times. The host and the crowd of this talk show are trying their best to not give him an awkward face, but you can tell that it's so hard for them not to…………………………...*

__Bold Face Liars---__ Interrogations have stepped up their tactics a lot further and somewhat more advanced than ever before. Just the sound and what you see that they use now have pushed people into telling, but lots of people have also died in the process as well. As we are actually in the room of a live interrogation as we speak, here I am for my first time seeing it and the equipment including the chairs are scary enough. If word got out about the things that are down here I'm pretty sure that this place would be shut down and many people would be sued and go to prison. A majority of the guys who work in this interrogation room are White and you have myself and this Mexican guy in here as well. The guy in the interrogation chair is a White guy that is breathing heavily and sweating so much that it's making my anxiety rise. I don't know what the straps and the chair is specifically doing to him, but he's terrified, but still not saying anything that's been of wanted information. That was until these 2 other White guys came into the room holding this heavy ass looking face molding device as they have big smiles on their faces. They both look at the guy seated in the chair and they say "You sure you don't want to tell us? Because that's fine by us. We've been dying to use this equipment again. The last guy we put this on told us what we wanted to hear, but we couldn't understand him because this face molder had suffocated him. Now one more time before we set this up. Are you going to tell us what we want and need to hear or do we need to mask you up?" That's when that shivering White guy in the interrogation seat shook his head telling them "No." I'm guessing he was calling their bluff, but I could tell that those 2 White guys holding the face molding was serious as fuhh about using it. They came in closer and that's when the Mexican guy asks them "What does that thing necessarily do?" That's when those 2 White guys looked up at him and I and said "Basically suffocates these ass holes. You will see since he wants to be a hard ass, but I'm holding the front of the face as a bisection and he is holding the back bisection of the head." As he points at the other guy that came in the room with him then continues on by saying "Whether your face matches this molding structure or not which all of time it doesn't, we screw in both sides around the hard asses face and the tighter we screw this magnificent invention the less and less oxygen he will have and whenever he doesn't tap out that's when the both of us let go of this device and depending on which way this device is leaning to the most all determines which way this will rip his head off due to how heavy this fucking thing is." That's when they smiled and one of the guys looked at the guy in the interrogation chair and said "I hope you're listening and paying attention because these are some of the last words you are going to hear before you die in this brutal way. There's only one way to survive this besides telling us what we need to hear, but we will tell you once you lose all oxygen and your head is *ripped off." As they put both ends of this metal face death contraption on him this Mexican guy and I are looking at one another like "What the fuhh?! This is some* **fuhdd** *up shit that no one should go through or even allow." No wonder why the security is so tight here. I already don't agree with what's going on here, but what the fuck am I to do or say as of now? As the metal face is being screwed in on this guys face I had to turn around as all of the White guys in this room were making sick comments and fuhdd up jokes. One guy saying "Such a "bold faced liar!" While just about everyone in this room started laughing as you could hear the guy in the interrogation room struggle and fight for oxygen and his life and you could hear him tapping repeatedly letting them know that he gave up and that he was willing to give up some information, but they ignored it and said "You wait! Too late!" Then they stepped back letting go of the metal face contraption and all you could hear was his neck break, blood gushing everywhere and spilling, and the loud clunk of the metal faced contraption hit the ground. All of those White guys were laughing and clapping and smiling at what had just happened and then they looked at me and the Mexican guy and said "OK. Fun part guys. The two of you have to clean up this mess and haul this body the fuck out of here. Oh yeah!" Then they looked at the headless body in the chair and the head inside of the metal face on the ground and they said "All you had to do was hold your breath for 20 seconds to unlock the mask automatically. Too late though." Then all of those White guys began laughing again as they looked at the Mexican guy and I as they were leaving out of the room and they said "Have fun!!"…………………………*

<u>Flying Penguins In Alaska---</u> *Here we are! My maintain and I are on another plane on yet another trip. Vacations are the best for us especially me as I'm working tremendously hard and don't know how to take a break, but I do ease up whenever I'm on vacation, but I still write. I do let my body heal though which is about the only time I do so besides the weekends and when my body and mind is just moving too slow. Anyways, as I'm by the window seat because I like to see how high above ground we are and because my maintain is afraid of the window seats, all I see is a lot of white. Like fog, clouds, and a lot of snow although we are in the air above the clouds. I really can't see much, but it's cool to be next to my maintain as we do this and go to Alaska for the first time ever together although it was supposed to be on a cruise ship, but it is what it is right now. No complaints, either way this is a trip and an experience to be a part of together and for new ideas, visions, and creativity to come. My maintain and I are talking and that's when her eyes had gotten all big as she looks past me to look out the window. I looked out the window and I was shocked with what I had seen. "What the fuhh?! Wow! Is this real? I never…" That's when I had seen hundreds and hundreds of penguins flying in the air by the plane. These penguins were by the pack and were flapping their wings, but were in the sitting position with their feet straight out ahead of them while doing so. I have never seen this before or even heard of this, this was incredibly unique. The only time I had seen penguins were in the zoo and even then the zoo keepers told us that they couldn't fly. Even in movies and in books we were told they could not fly. My maintain was in total shock, excitement, and disbelief. As soon as I was about to pull out my phone, that's when the airplane intercom had turned on and the pilot said "Ladies and gentlemen. We are now at our destination in Alaska and we are about to land now. Prepare for landing as we will be landing on snow and ice so it may be a little bumpy." I was so curious to why nothing was said about the penguins, but whatever. As we prepare to land my maintain and I have our phones out as we are recording the penguins* *outside of our window and that's when we landed a few moments later and the pilot was not joking about how bumpy this landing would be. As the whole plane is rattling and we are slowing down, that's when we had come to a complete stop as everyone had looked around and that's when…………………..*

<u>Ginger Snap Fired---</u> *So my job and the whole department had just left a huddle/meeting to go into another one. As all of us were moving to the same area none of us had masks on our faces which is definitely a good sign because that means that the pandemic is over. As we were leaving our department to a nearby department to bring the rest of the building together for a huge meeting, that's when the manager of my department had slowed down so that I would walk by her and she said to me "I'm probably about to get fired." I moved my head back and looked at her like "What the fuhh?!" And "Why would you be telling me of all people this?" And that's when………………………………*

<u>Jealousy Pro's---</u> *So there's this football player, for K-State specifically that is a sports phenom. This fool is from Colorado originally and had recruits from all over look at him for his record breaking and his athletic achievements. Not only is this buff tall Black guy athletically gifted, but he is academically gifted and special as well. All the way from Colorado Springs, Colorado and out of ALL of the universities he's been to even the top 3 in the whole country he has decided to come to Manhattan, Kansas to K-State Campus to be a WildCat in my hometown. Now due to his popularity and my popularity being the dumbbell guy and him seeing my style of workouts we have met through a mutual friend that is a huge college football fan, my daw T.B. After he had introduced us we have become cool and started talking a lot about life and what we have been through, what motivates us, and what we plan to do with the rest of our lives. It's beautiful because you never know who a person truly is until you hear the experiences they have encountered. Although he is from the state next to the middle of the map Kansas, no one has really known the dangers and death threats he has left. His talent and skill on the football field is beyond phenomenal as if there was no care in the world and that life was perfect, but now it makes sense to why he is so focused on the football field, it eliminates all of his worries when he let's go of all that aggression and frustration with his favorite sport. I can't believe that this guy has harbored all of this pain. We are talking more and more as we are in his apartment across the street from the K-State football field and I'm so in tune to help this guy out more and more, but I do verbally congratulate him for being such a humble guy. To still stay so focused academically and athletically even with all of the hate he's been dealt with from his hometown. Someway somehow they keep finding out his number and they're calling and leaving voicemails trying to mentally fuck him up. I asked him if he thought that these guys would ever come to Kansas to threaten him even more and that's when he had looked at me and said "I don't know. I'm sure if they found a way they would." That's when I then asked him "Why do you think they hate you so much?!" That's when he said "I know why they hate me so much! It's because I worked my ass off for a better life and created most of my opportunities and successes with less excuses and it makes them see the things that they can achieve, but they don't allow themselves to do. That's not my fault and that's not my responsibility. I'm living for me, my family, and the people that want to do better that are actually working to do so." That's when I said to him "I completely understand that my daw." Then that's when T.B. and I* *stood up and I asked the football player "Aye, you wanna go out to AggieVille with us and get something to eat?" That's when the football player stood up and said "Yeah. Thanks for the talk, it helps out a lot and I do need to get out. Let me change right quick." As he left the living room to go back into his room and this fool was literally gone for like 30 seconds, newly dressed and walking out towards us as he grabs his keys off of the kitchen table and he says "Let's goooooooo!!!!!" As we opened the front door to step out as we are on the 4th floor sitting high. I thought to myself "This has to suck during the winter going down." The football player locks his door then we go down the steps and I asked them "Where would y'all like to eat? There's a few places I know of in AggieVille. There's Burger King, Gordo's WingStop, Buffalo Wild Wings…...That's all I can think of right now." As we made it to the bottom of the staircase and we were deciding if we were all going to take the same vehicle together or separate rides, that's when this red car came driving by so fast in the parking lot and stopped and we all looked at it like "Who the fuhh is this?" Then we began laughing because we thought it was some college people trying to be funny that was until people jumped out of the car with black hoodies on and guns shooting at us and……………………………...*

Shirt Talk--- *It's myself along with Big Joke seated down in this classroom having a good talk about life and many things that we can't talk about or that we don't have enough time to talk about while at work. There's lots of things we were going over both funny and serious, that was until this fool Jafay came busting through the door with some shirts in his hands and he looked at us with this goofy ass look on his face and he says "Hi guys! What are y'all doing? Nevermind that! Let's talk shirts!" That's when Big Joke and I looked at one another like "What the fuck! OK! Whatever!" As Jafay drops his shirts on the desk right in front of him and he grabs a marker and starts writing some sloppy ass handwriting on the board and before he even finished writing the sentence he turns around real fast and says "Big Joke! What kind of things do you like to eat? Like favorite characters on your favorite cereal?" That's when Big Joke says "Honey Comb! I like Honey Comb!" Then Jafay turns back around and writes "Honey Comb" on the dry erase board and then Jafay says "See I like Frosted Flakes! I'm going to work up something in the lab and add both of these ideas to my shirts and y'all let me know what y'all think." As he grabs his shirts from off of that desk and he walks out of the classroom leaving his writing on the dry erase board I even think he took that marker with him and that's when……………...*

Battle Rap Talk With Pat Stay--- *So here is Pat Stay and I on his podcast as we are seated in a comfy chair across from one another and we are in a deep conversation about what we missed and loved so much about battle rap. Before battle rap had become so mainstream, controlled, and commercialized. It lost the substance and that authentic feel. It gets the same with music in all genres and entertainment in general. "When was the last time there was an actual classic song, movie, or battle recently? Anything of replay value? To me I feel like everything from ten or so years ago especially the early 2000s and the 90s etc. and beyond was when everything had more passion, creativity, and content in it." I said to Pat Stay as he looked at me with this big smile on his face and he said "I completely agree with you dude! Nothing is worth a great reaction or to save anymore. I don't know if there's so many people doing it now that everyone is saying the same stuff and sounding like the previous battlers that have been* *around for years or what?! It's ridiculous." That's when I said "Trueness. Many of these corporations picking up on it are ruining the feel and these platforms are literally selling out." That's when the both of us agreed and………………………………………………………*

What Happened To US?!--- *Here WE are. I don't know what the fuck happened, how, and why? This is ridiculous as fuhh. My maintain and I are in this beat up ass trailer and I'm at the front door as she's walking out of the room towards me and all of the guys sleeping and lounging around in the front room are all of the fools that have tried to be funny with my maintain knowing that she was in a relationship with me. Every single one of these fools. And my maintain is walking through as if there is no problem and as she steps closer and closer to me that's when my anxiety began rushing and with every step she was taking all I could feel and hear were the vibrations from each step. She stopped right in front of me and I shoved her as her eyes got all big. I couldn't believe that she would disrespect me like this. I'm so hurt and mad, but so hurt more than anything that I grabbed her with tears dropping from my eyes and I told her "Come the fuck outside! NOW!" I was so mad that I seriously didn't give a fuck about getting jumped or putting my hands on her. I'm so hurt, embarrassed, ashamed, and heart broken and she seems to not even care. We stepped outside in the snow that's left on the ground after most of it has melted as I walk away from her expecting for her to follow me as I got into my white Chevy Impala and sat down as she stood a few feet from the open door that's when I hit the steering wheel and said "Fuck! Fuck you! What the fuck are you doing?!" As I looked over at her and she had no emotion on her besides the fact that she looked annoyed and that's when she told me about how she had changed the rest of the bills in her name, but she emphasized the electric bill the most and that's when she then………………………………*

Chris Unbias At Calicoe's Calico--- *So I'm on the set holding the camera while we are in Detroit for an episode to interview the battle rapper Calicoe. I am surprised to see the neighborhood Calicoe lives in simply because I would have assumed after the years and years of battle rapping and his name and stature that he would have lived in a way better neighborhood in a nicer house, but I guess not, that's what I get or assuming. As Chris and the camera crew step up to the front porch that's when Chirs rings the doorbell uncontrollably until the music is turned down from within the home and we hear some guy yell out "HOLD THE FUCK UP! I'M COMING! SHIT!" As we wait outside for about 10 seconds after hearing that that's when we could hear the door locks unlock and the front door swing open aggressively and Calicoe is at the door as he notices Chris Unbias and cameras pointed on him and I guess that made him even more mad not knowing that that was going to be what was at his door. That's when Calicoe yells out "WHAT THE FUCK DO YOU HAVE ALL THESE FUCKING CAMERAS ON ME FOR??!!!!" Then that's when these feezies started running out of the front door past Calicoe and Chris Unbias, myself, and the other cameraman with us. Calicoe looks at them, then the cameras, and then us and he yells out "FUCK!!!!" And slams the door in front of us loud and hard as fuhh that he cracked the screen on the front door and that's when Chris Unbias, myself, and the other cameraman had looked at one another and we kept the cameras rolling as we stepped off the property and closer to the sidewalk and that's when Chris Unbias started saying "Well that didn't go any way the way we planned it to." Then that's when he hand signaled to me to hand him my camera so I did and Chris Unbias put the camera lens really* *close to his face and said something along the lines of "Calicoe is usually a cool......" then all of a sudden gun shots are being heard close to us as we were running away from Calicoe's house and then…………………………..*

The Spanish Cell Phone Guy--- *So I'm in this weird ass mall that is dark as fuhh as if I'm here past closing time or as if the lights had gone off. Which with all of the things that have been going on with Texas lately as in the past 3 years it could be either or, but more than likely the electricity had gone out. I'm outside of the store where the mall has flood lights within the hallways, but myself and this Spanish guy are very determined to make this transaction happen and go through. What's really weird is how I'm at this cell phone store when I have been using TracPhones for years because I've had a contract before and the customer service sucked and my bills were ranging from 2 times to 4 times as much as I'm paying now. Now my maintain and her family on the other hand are under a major cell phone provider's contract, but that's their business. Maybe that's what and who I'm here for. As this fool is on his phone speaking Spanish right in front of me I'm assuming he's getting business done and closing out the transaction as I'm standing in front of him as we are in this hallway and he's on this crate like box or whatnot with these very dark blue curtains on the side of him as if he's on a tiny stage on broadway. The more that he is speaking Spanish on the phone in front of me the more I can hear some lady's voice behind me getting closer and closer as I can feel and tell that she's like right behind me and that's when she smiles at me as she continues to speak Spanish on the phone then she smiles at the Spanish guy right in front of me. She then hangs up as she's speaking Spanish towards the end of the phone call and then that guy was speaking Spanglish as well as he hung up too. The Spanish lady is smiling really big and then she says in English "You're a very handsome man. The lights are already off and we should have some fun." That's when I put my fist to my mouth and smiled and turned around saying "Whewwwwwwww!!!! She looks good and she can speak English very well too!" That's when that Spanish guy looked at me and started laughing as the Spanish feezy had then grabbed my arm and pulled me away and that's when I was going to ask about my cell phone, but then I figured I would hold that off for another time after I figure out where this lady is taking me and what we are about to do……………………………………………………*

Left My Bag At Work?--- *So I'm at home having an anxiety attack trying to find my bag where I keep my raps, inventions, ideas, plans, dreams, books, and goals, but not seeing it anywhere in the house or in the car or our van. "What the fuck?! Where could I have put it? How did I fucking forget my bag of all things/" That's when I forced myself to stop where I was at and think about all of the places I have been to. "Where all have I been today? Think! Fuck! Work! Works where I've been! OK! Asiago!" As I began visualizing in my head what all I've done before I got off work and if I remembered grabbing it and that's when I remembered it being on the floor by my lunchbox and that's when I ran to the room to grab my keys and get ready to head back to work and……………………………………………………………..*

A Maverick In Dallas--- *Here I am for the first time in the city of Dallas, Texas. I've heard a lot about this place and here I am finally! After so many years of meeting people from Dallas that have moved to Kansas through the military or others that have been to Kansas or family* *members or even the K-State University college. Dallas, Houston, and Austin, Texas are the main places in Texas I have always had on my list to travel to especially Houston due to the huge DJ Screw, Screwed Up Click, SwishaHouse, Chopped and Screwed rap music scene I had grown up on. Here I am in Dallas though. I'm in front of a group of Mexican people both women and men and these are not relatives of my maintain. They are all suited up and very excited to see me as we are meeting to discuss a business deal for sports here in Texas, but obviously starting off with the city that means the most at this point which is Dallas! Now I'm not as big into basketball, football, or baseball as I was once, but I have planned to spread my business ventures deeper especially with my fitness apparel and motivation into a wider range of sports that gets the most amount of publicity and viewers. I used to be big into football before my teenage years and into my teenage years basketball was my favorite sport as I was a huge fan of the Houston Rockets when Tracy McGrady played. After high school I got really big into fighting such as MMA/UFC and a little bit of boxing, but mainly old school boxing matches. Let's get back to the point though. As we are all seated in this conference room giving good energy, everyone is in a good mood feeling free and comfortable, that's when papers are passed around the table and I then heard a friendly and thick Mexican accent ask me "So you want to buy the Dallas Mavericks first mi amigo?" That's when I looked around at everyone with a big confident smile and said "Yuh, yuh I do!" As everyone had smiled at me and then we………………………..*

Marketing The Stock Market--- *Big business talks! I have literally been investing my time into the stock market as of lately and when I say "As of lately" I mean in the past 3 or so years. I have become so dedicated in the multiple income making money streams and how to flip money and become the best entrepreneur that I can be, that I have taken it an elevator further and moved my way to working corporate on Wall Street until I can learn so much that I am my own corporation living by my own rules. Right now I am suited up watching the stocks with a whole bunch of other suited up people as well. The diversity in the stock market culturally is a lot more than what people generally think. There are so many different races and a lot of women here as well. I've been linking up with some prominent people in this field and my account has been showing that. So here we all stand gathered together as we are getting ready to make even more money………………………………………*

The Roller Blader Trainer--- *So I'm in my hometown of Manhattan, Kansas aka Wild City, Kanziss in the parking lot of The Holidae Inn and waiting on someone as I'm seated in the driver's seat listening to music as cars driver by. It's around rush hour and lots of cars are driving by and I'm just thinking about how busy the city can be and how busy it has especially gotten in the past 10 years and how much bigger it's going to get. The amount of cars driving by is giving off a nice gust of wind that feels so good. As I've been listening to Lloyd Banks, Mook Boy, and Big L as I'm just seated and waiting, that's when I see a fool I haven't seen in months drive by and I know he had to have seen me, but he's refusing to give me eye contact, this fool Camble. Which we were really cool at one point until this fool built up some envy and started acting funny though no one else is laughing. I'm staring at this fool, but he's fake zoning out so he doesn't have to look at me until he goes right through the light. I'm thinking to myself "I don't get that fool?" I tried linking up and helping him, but yet he still acts funny. Fuck it!" Then I go back to listening to music until a few moments later some buff ass Black fool comes* *by rollerblading and he's big as fuhh. To be honest this fool might even be bigger than me. Up top this fool is rounded and big as he's shirtless and he comes rollerblading fast. I see his grey sweat pants and you could just tell from the thickness of his legs is ridiculous as well. This guy was big as fuhh! Guess what was going on though? Not only was this fool big and was rollerblading, but he had 100 pound dumbbells in each hand as he was bicep curling with rollerblades on. This guy took the or should I say "MY" dumbbell walk to a whole other extreme. I have never seen anything like this or ever imagined someone modifying my work out like this. As he is bicep curling and rollerblading down the block and I'm standing up outside of my car watching him there's a camera crew following him and recording all of this which explains the microphone piece to his mouth and he's explaining the work out as he's working out and………………………………...*

College Party Stinker--- *So I'm at this big ass house during a college party with people running and moving around everywhere. The music is going and playing all kinds of genres, but mainly rap. People are moving everywhere and drinking everywhere. It's a good time to vibe along and have a good time with everyone. I go to the restroom right quick and this restroom is huge. It's big enough to have it's own house or to be a room itself and frazy thing is that there's only one big ass bathtub and one big ass toilet in here and a sink, mirror, etc. but for the size of this restroom you would assume that there would be more tubs and toilets and sinks and maybe even some urinals, but I guess not. I go to sit on the toilet thinking I had to shit, but I guess not. I'm sitting on the toilet still though relaxing and thinking about life as I could hear the music in the background, conversations, and people laughing. "I'm glad that I get out the house more." I'm thinking to myself as I slowly sat up pulling my boxers and sweatpants up. I walk out of the restroom and back through the living room to look out the sliding door and seeing a whole bunch of college people in the backyard partying harder than the people inside. Some people are streaking, some are shirtless even the feezies. Some feezies with just a bra on and some shorts and some just completely naked. "I LOVE K-STATE!" I say out loud as everyone puts their cups in the air and cheers. I go outside and there's a big ass pool with fog on the water that goes hard! Lights in the pool and the backyard that makes it look even more fun. I notice some of the fools here from my dumbbell walk I do as I've taken pictures with them as they always cheer me on when I walk by them. They're waving at me smiling and saying "What's up?" to me as they come towards me until they get real close when they give me this look as if something or someone stinks, particularly myself. They backed away and moved away slowly and that's when I looked around and then I looked down as somehow my clothes had disappeared and my dick was hard and not only did I smell like shit, but I had shit on me. I jumped as I noticed that and I looked up to notice people look at me and that's when I looked around and debated on jumping into the pool to get this shit off me or to take a shower at this party and that's when I decided to…………………………………...*

Called An Idiot By The Boss--- *So I don't know when, why, or how, but my job had moved all of their operations into this mansion. Where the whole company's employees were basically at was the library of this mansion and we were doing everything from dusting, mopping, sweeping, rearranging books, moving books, etc. Not in that order, but a lot of stuff was getting done. I'm walking through these bookshelves which were so big that this library was bigger than the* *warehouse from the building we just had transferred from. As I'm walking through the bookshelves there's this older tatted dub dub that has a nice ass and she looks really good for her age that is very nice to me and I wouldn't mind smashing. She's ahead of me pushing a cart of books and a book drops off of the cart so she stops to bend over and get it and that's when the ass cheeks part of her black yogas had spread, not ripped, but spread open and showed the fatness of her pussy from the back in that pink and polka dot white thong. Dizzamn! That looked so good and a sight I didn't mind seeing. That's when this skinny dub dub with black hair that's tatted as well ran past me and towards the polka dot thong dub dub and said "Awe!" As she gasped and the polka dot thong dub dub stood up to put the book bag on her cart then turned around slowly to look at me as she smiled and then she saw the skinny dark haired dub dub run towards her and she had said something lightly to her as they had walked away turning left to the next aisle. I continued to walk through the aisle to go to where I had seen Ginger Snap and Dani and even Casondra as I grabbed a mop bucket to mop up this open area until I saw that someone had dumped a whole bucket of black ink everywhere and they had even had their hand prints all over it too. I'm looking at them and the black paint everywhere like "What the fuck?! This just so happens to be here when I grabbed this mop and bucket, but wasn't when I was in the aisle with the books." I said. I'm confused to why they are just staring at it. Since I'm the one with the mop and bucket I guess it's on me to do this as I pull the wet mop from the bucket water and into the wringer to wring it out and putting the mop on the ground into the ink as the 3 of them continue to stare at the floor that's when I say "I can't believe there's fucking hand prints in this shit! Someone did this on purpose!" And as I'm talking about this that's when Ginger Snap tries to butt in , but I'm not going to allow her to talk to me like that so I continued to talk over her and she stopped and I said "There's handprints everywhere! Where's the person that did this? Y'all don't see these prints everywhere?" That's when her face had turned red and I knew that something was up and that's when she yelled out at me "JUST MOP IT UP! YOU FUCKING IDIOT!!!" That's when I had looked at her with that "Are you fucking frazy?!?!" look. She was serious as she was breathing heavily and Casondra looking at me as if she was on Ginger Snap's side and Ginger Snap looking at me as if she's been wanting to say that for a while now. As much as I tried to not let what she said bother me I couldn't get over the fact that as my manager/boss if I would have said that to her it would have been a bigger problem, but the look she's giving me and the double standards I couldn't hold back anymore so I dropped the broomstick and yelled in her face "ARE YOU FUCKING SERIOUS!!!! FUCK YOU! FUCK YOU!!!" As I shoved her so fucking hard that it hurt my shoulders as she slid back a few feet, but didn't fall at all. That's when Casondra stepped up until this buff ass Hawaiian guy had busted through these huge wooden oak doors and I noticed him as being a boxer on my GramInsta page and he's charging towards me as I'm yelling out "KNOW THE FUCKING STORY! KNOW THE FUCKING STORY!" As he stopped to think about that and I walked away mad as fuhh to go past the bookshelves and by the staircase as the sun beamed brightly through the windows and I began to walk up the steps and……………...*

<u>Dick To The Left---</u> *Here I am in the bathroom of my home after waking up from a sore ass sleep. I have been working out so hardcore that I've even been doing hardcore and full body exercises that make me contemplate not getting out of my bed at times. I am so fucking sore, but I've still got to wake all the way up and stay up because I have to write in my books and I've* *got to also write these songs while everyone stays asleep due to less distractions. As I'm sitting on the toilet and taking a piss because I am so tired I have to hold my dick down because it's hard and because I don't want it to touch the toilet. The more I hold it down the weaker the stream so I stay seated until I'm done taking a piss then I stand up and I turn the bathroom light on. My dick is so hard that I've got to look down to see what's going on with it. I look down and I see how my dick is super long and super hard, but it's "cocked" to the left. I pull it towards the middle and there's some resistance in it as when I let go it went back to the left . I'm thinking to myself "What the fuhh?!" As I'm thinking "Is my dick going to permanently stay like this? Is this from me jacking off all of the time? What do I do?"..*

The Shugliest Race Question--- *So I'm on a live set performance of this TV game show called "What The Fun?!" that asks the contestants a whole bunch of questions that are random and so off the wall that many people end up never winning because they do not want to offend a whole group of people and deal with the national criticism and because many of these questions are uncomfortable and they always seem to get uncomfortable the more and more as the show progresses and more and more episodes are made. One contestant was 2 questions away from winning over $2 million dollars until one of the questions he had to answer was "Does your wife's pussy ever stink?" The guy looked at his wife and she looked so embarrassed and he decided to drop out of the show right then and there. Another person was then asked "Are you not excited to to fuck your husband? Do you think about him getting it over with already? Have you thought about fucking his friends?" and "Is it trueness that you've been fucked way better by other's before, during, and after your husband?" She became another TV show drop out. Many of these clips and episodes go viral from the internet to the news. You have either got to answer the questions presented to you or you have got to drop out. So here I am as a contestant on the show and the question on the board that looks like how it looks on Family Feud is "Which race of people have the shugliest people?" That's when everyone looks around super uncomfortable because this isn't just an in home close friends and family conversation this is on national TV and millions of people are watching which means millions of people are going to get offended if this question gets answered. For the chance to win $10 million dollars I'm going to answer this and apologize later because I cannot specifically clarify this answer while on air. That's when I say out loud "Well every race has some shugly ass people in it, but that doesn't make the whole race shugly. Now if this was a question of which race has the most beautiful women it would be easier to answer." As I let out a deep breath and looked around and thought about all of the things I could buy, see, and do for my family with being a millionaire and that's when I said "The shugliest race of people from my experience and haven't gotten many dates would have to be…………………………………………*

Night Time Neighbors--- *Here I am stepping outside on my new wide wooden front porch to enjoy the nice calm night breeze as the summer time is moving into fall. It's dark and the wind feels great. As I'm just standing in the wind and just looking around, that's when I see this car drive by slow, but it's hard to tell what color it was exactly because I didn't have my porch light on and this street is pretty dark. All I know is that the car was dark. This car was anywhere from the color black to maybe dark blue or red. I'm not sure. The car drove by slowly and then a few seconds later this pastor guy came walking into the grass. Now when I say this pastor* *guy I mean the guy I met and became friends with due to him seeing me work out outside and saying that I'm inspiring. It's weird though that he knew where I lived and even weirder knowing that he's walking up to my home and my porch when it's almost midnight. I pulled out my phone just to double check to see what time it was and my phone showed "12:13am." I'm thinking "What the fuck?!" And that's when I got a notification through BaceFook that my neighbor had taken a picture of a soda in his hand as his maintain was across the room, maybe in the kitchen taking a picture of him. I thought to myself "When did we become BaceFook friends? Last time I checked we were connected by him being on my fan page." A lot of off the wall abnormal and weird shit is going on right now and I don't know what to say to the Pastor because I only came outside for a few minutes to feel the breeze then to go back inside to relax and go to sleep. I liked my neighbors' picture on BaceFook and then that's when I heard my neighbors front door open and then screen door open and foot steps off their porch and onto the grass and that's when I saw my neighborhood and his maintain walk towards my porch and that's when…………………...*

The Family Reunion--- *So a bunch of my family has come to Kansas all the way from North Carolina for a huge family reunion. Due to many family members passing we have decided to come together to see one another and not take the time or the distance for granted no longer. I'm so surprised though because so many of my family members live in North Carolina so for them to all travel here was a good deed, blessing, and reward. We are all gathered up at my aunt's house in her backyard as we barbecue, have music playing loudly, and just having a good time laughing, cracking jokes, reminiscing, hugging, and taking pictures with one another. This was probably the first time in a while and when I say a while I mean almost 10 years or so since myself and all 4 of my sisters have been together in the same space. Now I haven't talked to my mom or seen her in almost 2 years now and if and when I see her at this party I seriously don't know what I'mma say to her or if I even want to say anything to her. The last time we spoke was an all out argument that lead to me snapping because she had used me and my friends help to move all of her stuff and my stuff out of the storage unit we shared and then with me not even having my own permanent place to stay or money for a storage unit she told me to get ALL of my shit out of her apartment the day after and didn't give a fuck if there was a place for it or not. I felt so used that day and she refused to see it from my point of view and never apologized or could admit that what she did was wrong. Now last I heard my mom's health has gotten worse due to all of her drinking and not taking care of her diabetes as well. I've helped her out and gave her as much advice as I could, but she just doesn't want to help herself as much as she says she does. So as I'm walking through this reunion smiling and having a good time that's when I see my mom smiling at me as if she is excited to see me. She's seated on this green and white striped lawn chair and looking at me as if we had never had a problem. As if I forgot or that I should forget about all of the pain she has given me over the years, but yet she won't let go of anything! It's always like this, but I'm tired of it. I see her and I walk away and…………………………………...*

All The Black Guys Hit On Me--- *So my maintain and I have been arguing back and forth for weeks now and it's getting tiring. Her insecurities from the beginning of our relationship have gotten the best of me and have rubbed off on me. From where we go and from who we have on* *social media has become such a problem that it's like we can't even have fun anymore. I've been accused of dumb ass shit all because of her insecurities but when I found out she had a condom in her wallet and she tries to explain it by saying she liked the wrapper and that it's not what it looks like. Even if she is telling the truth it still looks like what it looks like to me and I feel as if these are red flags that I'm easily ignoring or trying to convince to not look at like that. From all of the back and forth arguing between her and I and the insecurities this has just made things worse. I don't believe what she says and I can't trust her wherever she goes which used to never be a problem at all. If her and her boss text which he is a guy I feel a certain way about it. Whenever she hangs out with her friends especially if they are her single friends I will feel sour about that as well. It's even gotten to the point where I told her "I don't even trust you going to work now and I feel like you're going to be talking to fools there." Guess what she tells me after I say that? "All the Black guys hit on me at work." I can't be mad at her for being honest with me, but it makes me wonder if she's been flirting back especially with all of the arguing going on between her and I lately. I'm so stressed and as much as I love her I refuse to go through this drama and pain any longer and the respect and integrity I have for myself is way more than dealing with this shit. That's when I decided to make my decision and I………………..*

DayLyt's Porn--- *So I'm watching a battle rap notification that has popped up on my phone saying "DayLyt versus Murda Mook" which this is a huge battle with 2 very solidified battle rappers that have earned their spots and are very lyrical rappers. This battle is so big and long awaited for the battle rap community that everyone is so surprised that this battle was uploaded to YouTube and not the World's Most Respected app. I'm so excited to see this battle as this battle is the battle that has been talked about for years, but was never really locked in and no one ever really thought it would happen. This title alone is historical and I know everyone is wondering what kind of off the wall stuff DayLyt had planned for this battle that was until the battle had got to where nothing has been seen or heard before on stage during a live event. DayLyt is rapping incredibly intricate and unique with multis, double and triple entendres, similes, metaphors, and a scheme about sex, getting fucked, and porn rhyming "torn," and "born," and "worn" with "warn" and then that's when DayLyt says "Stop my time. Yo! Stop my time!" As he steps to the edge of the stage and gives off this long speech about porn and how sinful it is and how we shouldn't be watching or recording other people or ourselves have sex. He is preaching to the crowd and him preaching is getting as much of a reaction as his raps were and no ones ever seen or heard of this before especially at or in a battle event. Then after his speech DayLyt goes back to saying "light, start that time again!" Then he starts rapping and scheming about the time we have in our life and the energy and life and everyone is reacting uncontrollably as this first round is already historical and talked about. DayLyt did not come to play! Every bar is phenomenal as this round is going to have to be topped or somewhat matched somehow with something very nice when it's Murda Mook's time to rap and that's when…………………………………....*

<u>A Bed & A Wrinkled Forehead</u>--- *So it's my maintain, this feezy that I went to high school with named Trinity Cup, and I moving a bed out of this room of this house we are moving out of. This mattress is the California King my maintain and I have been trying to get for awhile now and finally got. After the hours of sweating and constant moving our stuff out of this house for a* *new and improved one that we are so excited about that's when we got to where we are at now at this point in time and that's moving this California King size mattress out with myself on one end and my maintain and Trinity Cup on the other end. This mattress is bigger, thicker, and wider than most beds so it's difficult to maneuver for me so I can only imagine how it is for the 2 women on the other end. The side of the mattress that's pointing up to the ceiling is wobbling and folding all over the place and bending as we are trying to move. Everyone's getting frustrated and this would be so much easier if we had one more person in the middle to at least keep the top part straight to not make this so difficult to move it through the door frame to get it out of the room. We have to keep moving slightly then put the mattress down because it's getting too heavy for everyone. After about the 4th time of putting the mattress down and we're already frustrated that's when Trinity Cup drops her side and yells out "Fuck this! Fuck this bed! And fuck your wrinkled forehead!" As she storms out of the room my maintain and I look at one another like "What the fuhh?!" Then we heard the slam of a door and…………………………*

That Shitty Cat--- *I wake up from a well needed and long nights sleep after my body has been screaming for a break as of late. As I'm waking up I feel that my maintain is not in the bed. I moved around and popped up quick from the bed to see the light in our bathroom on and I heard water move in the tub as some water slowly began to come out of the faucet and fill the tub. I move out of the bed and stepped off to put my feet in my flip flops as I stepped to the bathroom. As I'm stepping closer and closer to the bathroom I saw some shit on the floor by my dirty clothes bag and my dresser. I walk into the doorway of our bathroom to see my maintain naked in the bathtub with water flowing and she smiles at me with her big ass titties out in the open and that tight pussy out and breathing. I look at the tub and by the faucet there's another pile of shit in the tub and I looked at my maintain and I say "This cat has been shitting everywhere. There's even shit in the tub!" That's when my maintain sees the shit and tries to kick it not thinking about the water in the tub and the shit sloshes and mixes into the water as my maintain and I both yell "UGH!" out loud and I leaned back and looked behind me by the toilet and I see a lot of shit that's dry by the toilet and that's when I yell out "This cat has to fucking go!"...................*

Lava Level--- *So I'm myself in this video game with my shirt off and super buff and lean as I'm in this deep castle like limestone pit with lava that rises every so often. As I'm at the bottom I have to find a way to cross over the lava and run up steps and also climb to the top and the front of the castle to go further to my missions to beat this game. I have already failed once with the lava burning my heels into the cement and slowly covering me up as the lava burns me up and I have to restart and here I am looking around for a new way to approach this level and here I go……………………*

Moved My Car?--- *So it's early as fuhh in the morning and my maintain, my momster in law, and I are at the SouthSide gas station in my hometown of Manhattan, Kansas aka Wild City, Kanziss and we were all in such a rush that I am just now noticing that I put on my shoes and sweats for work along with my socks and boxers of course, but I forgot my fucking shirt. I looked at my maintain and my momster in law and I say "How the fuck did I forget my shirt of all things for work! It's still early enough so we have enough time to go back to the house to get* *my shirt so that I don't have to show up late and stay later." Then that's when I looked at both of them and then my car as the window is rolled down and the car was still running and at this time we literally lived over across the tracks on the other side of Fort Riley Boulevard. I then say "Can I hop in with y'all and y'all take me to the house right quick?" That's when they looked at me and said "Come on. Of course." So I opened the sliding door to the van and jumped in right quick as we drove off for a little bit and that's when headlights flashed behind us and I said "Stop the van. Stop the van!" I got out of the van as my maintain and her mom looked around like "What the fuhh?!" I'm looking back at the gas pump where I left my car and my car is gone. "What the fuhh?! Someone took my car!" I look around and I see if it's at another pump or a parking spot, but naw it's not. I look around on Fort Riley Boulevard and nothing. I then look towards the car wash and there my car is! But royal blue! Some tall White guy gets out of my car walking towards me and as he's approaching me I'm debating on whether cussing this fool the fuck out or if I should thank him. He's getting closer as he has a smile on his face and my keys in his hand and that's when……………………………………*

<u>Triple Nipple Wet Threat</u>--- *I'm waking up in this unfamiliar bed in this unfamiliar house next to one of my feezy friends Heila. This is weird because I haven't talked to her in almost a year verbally or through text or call. I'm waking up with not much time to yawn or stretch and she's already grabbing my face and making out with me and I'm looking around as I'm waking up more and I pull my body away from her and I get up from the bed and I ask her "How did I get here? Where's my girl at?" As she gave me this dumb look that's when I got up from the bed and left to the restroom, but it was a smaller room before the restroom and that's when this African girl launches her body onto mines and starts licking my face and kissing and sucking on my neck until I pulled her off of me to rush right into the restroom and shut the door behind me and locked it breathing heavily with my head up towards the ceiling and as soon as I opened my eyes to look around that's when I saw my momster in law rushing in towards me and I………………....*

<u>Lunch Break Clothes</u>--- *So I'm stepping out of this building in the downtown portion of Manhattan, Kansas aka Wild City, Kanziss that I have not seen before. From this angle it's beautiful and obviously I have a new job now with a longer lunch break and a less stressful setting. I have Wal-Mart bags with my basketball shorts and some shirts and my youngest son's cups for some reason. I step onto the nice red brick sidewalk as I look down the sidewalk and I feel the warm spring weather and the breeze of the wind against my skin as it feels so great to get some fresh air and natural light and being outside of a building after so many hours. I walked down the sidewalk for a little bit until I reached my bike as I pulled my bike out more and I sat on the seat and I began to ride my bike towards the crosswalk and traffic light on my way to my friend Scarie's house as she had finally moved to Manhattan. To be honest as I'm riding my bike and it's so relaxing, smooth, and peaceful I'm thinking about why I'm going to Scarie's house of all places then I get to thinking about all of the food I could eat there while on break and also how I could just see her and her new place for a little bit and not be convinced to stay and talk for hours since I have to be back to work as well. As I'm riding my bike away from downtown and towards the address she had given me the week she made her move I'm thinking about how riding our bikes was such a normal thing to do back then when we were* *younger and how much fun it used to be. How much exercise we would do on the daily as kids besides basketball at the D.C. almost everyday and besides school P.E. or intramurals. I know that if most of us were to keep bikes and would get out of the house more and stop depending on our cars so much that many of us would be in way better shape than we are now. Here I am though. Pulling up to Scarie's house which almost looks like the same house she had literally just moved out of in that other town she was in for years which I wonder if it was. I rode my bike up the rocky driveway until I got close to the front door which was literally a side door, but still. I knocked on the door as I heard heavy footsteps throughout the house and someone yell out "Coming! Hold on. Hold on. I'm coming!" As footsteps were getting closer and closer to the door and the curtain moved out of the way and it was my friend Scarie with a big smile on her face being so excited to see me. Her eyes are big and she invites me in her house where I see all of her boys in the kitchen portion of the house and her 2 oldest boys are big as fuhh. Weigh more and are taller than me both by A LOT! They all waved at me as I waved back and they're looking at the bags in my hands. Scarie pulls me to show me the tour of her "new" house and I tell her "This house looks exactly like the last one did, well from the outside as least." This house is pretty nice though better than the last one from the inside. She wanted to show me the upstairs and the basement, but I told her that I would check it out next time since I'm on my lunch break right now. Her two oldest sons were acting weird as fuhh though and usually the oldest one is the coolest as I've been around him plenty of times, but this time it's as if he wants to say "FUCK YOU!" to me and fight me. As I'm walking towards the front door I'm thinking to myself "Dizzamn! I'm hungry as fuhh! I at least could leave with a snack from here right?" But as I'm being walked out by Scarie that's when I was going to wave, but when I waved I had remembered the bags I had in my hands and that's when I say "Oh yuh. I have some stuff for your boys!" That's when the second oldest which he is the biggest and tallest, had rushed towards me and the door where his mom was at as well and he said "What do you have? What do you have?" As he snatched one bag from me and I looked at him with that "That was rude as fuhh" face, but he didn't care as long as there was a possibility of him having something he would take it and not say thank you. Scarie is smiling at him as if he cannot do any wrong and as he goes through the bag he is literally tossing the things to the side that need to stay in the bag like my son's cups for instance. He then pulls out my red basketball shorts and says "Yeah! Now that's what I'm talking about! I want these!" But those shorts aren't to be given away I looked at his mom and then back to him and he already had my shorts on that quickly and that's when I yelled out "Those aren't going! Those are mine! You can have something else in the bag, but not those my daw." That's when he was already turned around and walking away slowly moving his arms as if he thought he was cool and not wanting to listen to someone tell him "NO!" You could tell that these young fucks walked all over their mom, but they're not going to play that shit with me. I looked at his mom as she smiled in nervousness and I looked back at her son as I puffed up from all the air I was sucking in to get ready to yell at this bitch ass kid and that's when... the door slammed in my face and………………………………*

<u>In This House---</u> *I'm in this house. This huge ass big open house with no furniture, carpet, or decor that I can see from where I'm at as of now as it's dark as fuhh in here. I can see a bit of the wood floor that I'm standing on and a long wide wooden stair well, but that's about it. I don't know what I'm doing here or how I got here, but dizzamn I'm kind of scared because I don't* *know what else or who else is in here, but I'm going to have to control this fear to get out of here and figure out what the fuck is going on. I don't know what waits for me around a corner, in the darkness, up the steps or anywhere else throughout this house, but I have to prepare and if whatever or whoever is waiting on me to come their direction they better be strong, smart, and wise enough to prepare for me…………………………………………...*

KelMac's Son--- *Here I am walking into Wal-Mart in my hometown of Manhattan, Kansas aka Wild City, Kanziss on this hot and sunny summer day. As I'm walking in I see this older Mexican woman with this younger Mexican boy about 9 or so at least years old walking out of the store. As they are walking towards me I'm looking at the older Mexy lady and she's giving me this look of "Who the fuhh are you and what the fuhh are you wearing?" look as I stopped in front of them and I asked that little boy "Aye! You're KelMac's son right?" He looked up at me and he said "Yes!" And that's when I say "I was friends with your mom. How is she doing?" That's when that Mexy lady touches her grandson's back and pushes him out of the way as she walked past me and gives me a dirty look looking at me up and down and that's when I looked at her like "What the fuhh is your problem?" As I walked further into the store I noticed more and more people looking at me as I looked around and then looked down to see that I was dressed in a red see through plastic like rain coat through the store exposing my body and………………...*

Ogden Car Chase & Hide Out?--- *Here we are, my maintain and I walking out of the Liberty gas station in Ogden, Kansas. This gas station was supposedly shut down years ago, but here we are walking out of the active up and running gas station with drinks and snacks in our hands. It's late night literally after it was just broad day before we had crossed the street. As we are walking across the street to our van that is near the Ogden post office we hear sirens blare from the distance and we look at one another like "Dizzamn! What the fuck is going on in Ogden today?!" We got in the van and we put our drinks and snacks up as we reversed out and went down the main street until we heard those sirens up really close on us and that's when we had taken a turn down the little strip of narrow alley between the downtown post office and some storage units. The cops roll by us super slow and then they sped up as the sirens were sounding off further away then that's when our van then breaks down out of nowhere. "What the fuck?! The van won't put any gas through!" My maintain looks at me concerned as I hopped out of the van and told her that I was going to push it through the alley and she has to steer it until we can get it in a safe place and call her dad or someone to help us out and although it's dark as fuhh out here and something is going on in Ogden that we don't know about, but obviously it sounds like some serious shit that's when we…………………………...*

T-Gath Is Out--- *Here I am at my boring ass job that I'm working hard to get the fuck out of. I'm at my screen print machine and I was told that we are getting some new people in the department to help us out now that business is picking back up. Nothing really new to me as we have been here before and I've seen so many people come and go. As I walk by the dryer and I lean my arms against it to take some pressure off of my back from standing on the cement for hours that's when I feel someone stand next to me so I look over and it's one of the last people I had expected to see here or in Manhattan aka Wild City outside of his home in such a long time.*

T-Gath. Right beside me doing the same thing I'm doing as he has his hands on the dryer looking straight ahead as he has a lot on his mind, but doesn't know how to start his conversation. I know what T-Gath has done during the whole heroin bust in Manhattan which to me made me lose so much respect for him simply because ever since I have know him he has put on this front as if he was the toughest guy ever and because he's not from Manhattan, but everyone's tough before they are put into a tough ass situation right? Yuh, I heard he snitched and that's probably why he is acting the way he is now, but I'm not here to completely treat him as if he's a piece of shit, but I know we will talk about this situation as we work together. There's always people's reasons in a story and what I've heard about him does not include him it was just about him so we will have to talk about it as we work together and that's when T-Gath says…………………….....

Glenn Disrespect--- *So for some weird ass reason my maintain, our 2 boys, and I are at one of my old maintenance man's house named Glenn. This fool is so funny though. I met him years ago as he was fixing some apartment not too far from my roommate and I's at the time and he would always hit on this blonde dub dub that I was smashing at the time and trying to get to smash her and take her out to eat, you know, trying to be her sugar daddy and all. As we are all in his front room that's when Glenn starts talking to my maintain and spitting game to her, being disrespectful as fuhh and not giving a fuhh that I'm here or that my maintain is my maintain and in a relationship with me. He's asking to take her out to eat and buying this and that for her and that's when I yell out "WHAT THE FUCK MY DAW?! ARE YOU FUCKING SERIOUS? DISRESPECTFUL!" That's when Glenn then says "What? How?! I'm just telling her how beautiful she is and giving her a compliment. What's wrong with that? I can't take her out to eat?!" That's when I then say "She's in a relationship and that person is me! How about I fuck YOUR wife and give her back to you whenever I'm done?! How about that?!" That's when my maintain gives me this "Are you fucking serious?!" look and Glenn looks at me and says "Whoa! That's not even the same fucking thing!" That's when this young White couple comes in the door and walks upstairs and the White girl says "He's right! That's disrespectful! I'm with you on that one!" As she points at me as her boyfriend still goes up the steps not wanting to be involved in the situation maybe because that guy was Glenn's son. When that dub dub had taken my side that's when I looked at her, pointed, and smiled and said "See! Even she knows that's fucked up!" That's when she waves and goes up the steps and I yell out to my maintain and our boys "LET'S GO! NOW! LET'S FUCKING GO!" As they all got up and followed me to the door as Glenn gave me this dirty look as everyone walked past him as I had the screen door open ready for us to all leave together. As everyone had stepped out the front door that's when that dub dub had come back down the steps and said…………………………*

The Burning Holes--- *So I'm working at this site that has these burning holes that require you putting sticks in them to keep the fire going. There is a circular gated like sewer cap with four sections that allow you to have hand room to put sticks into the hole to keep it burning in what seems to look like a part of the SouthWest region of the United States maybe around Arizona or New Mexico or something. It was like a landfill and tourist attraction of geysers, but with small natural fire pits. As there are so many tourists around, I along with my coworkers are putting sticks into the fire as I am looking at these pits and I can see how dangerous this can be if* *someone was to fall or step into these things. After putting a couple of sticks into my pit I stand up and I brush myself off and I walk over to another pit as I squatted down to put more sticks into this pit as I look from afar and see some cliffs, nice craters, and nice landforms as I feel the breeze of the wind and some dirt hit my face and the heat from the pit and that's when…………..*

<u>Huge RoadSide Tire---</u> *So my maintain and I are in this car going down this road that looks like it could be Colorado somewhere. The road is beautiful with all of these hills and red dirt. As I'm driving down this hill we see this huge tire on the side of the road that is a monument and something we have never seen before that I told my maintain "I gotta get a picture next to that big ass tire!" That's when my maintain says "Let's take it then!" As we went down the hill some more getting closer and closer to that tire until we passed it so that we could park a little bit ahead of it. We got out of our seats and out of the car and we walked towards this tire as my maintain pulls out her iPhone and I walk closer and closer to the tire and cars are passing us and looking at us as if we are weird as fuhh, but this picture is going to look cool. As I got up real close to the tire that's when I realized that this was a real rubber tire with the rim and all. I was rubbing the tread of the tire and it blew my mind to know that this tire was real, but supersized. That's when my maintain yells out "Are you ready?" That's when I get my pose ready with a front double bicep and I yell back "Yuh! I'm ready!" And my maintain yells back "OK! Here I go!" She took the picture and that's when I switched to another pose just joking as if I was going to push the tire off of the structure it was molded to on the bottom, but the tire rolled off as I gasped and my maintain had gasped loudly and the tire rolled off down the hill past traffic and it was picking up so much speed as it was going down the hill and then………….*

<u>Madonna's Suicide---</u> *Here I am in what appears to be a movie where I come into a room into this big house with some people I have known for years. Everyone is crying as they're holding one another's hands and looking at me as I came into the room as I was told that something bad has happened to Maddona. Everyone is so emotional and drenched in tears that it's so hard for them to even explain what has exactly happened. I'm looking around seeing if anyone can tell me what's going on because I don't want to make any assumptions and be completely wrong and I make this situation worse off of an assumption. I walk out of the room where everyone is at and I go down the hallway just to leave all of that sorrow and low energy. I walk into the first room I see to my right where the door is cracked open and there's a dub dub in here and she's looking at the ground as she's sitting on the edge of the bed, but on the ground I see a body that's laying motionless. I step in the room more and more to see that this looks like it was the room Maddona was staying in and all over the room in black marker had "I Love Will" written all over the place which to me was already weird and obsessive looking, but what made it even more weird was the fact that Maddona was dating a fool named Chuck at the time. Now when I say that "I Love Will" was written all over the room I meant it. The more and more that I walk in the more and more that I see it everywhere! Literally from the floor to the furniture, the walls, and the ceiling. I stepped closer and closer to the dub dub in the room that's next to the motionless body on the floor and I noticed and recognized who that motionless body was. It was Maddona. Maddona is on the floor unresponsive as everyone in the house mourns for her* *and I'm not even sure if anyone has called for help as I stepped back seeing "I Love Will" written more and more and I………………*

Fail Vids Shit Talk--- *So my maintain and I are laying down about ready to end our day while putting on a compilation of viral fails on the TV just to have some background noise before we go to bed. This whole week and the weekend has been ridiculously fast and short. We've been on the go for the whole week with barely any time to relax at all. It's sad, but you know you've been productive and on the go when the only time you get to relax is when you are about to go to sleep. It puts a lot on the body and mind when you don't give yourself time to relax and heal. Anyways, as we are laying in bed with the compilations playing that's when one of the videos plays and some White guy is responding back to another White guy that was talking shit about the fails so the guy defending himself says out loud and aggressively "If that's how you feel about your fails then you can upload your successful attempts elsewhere! This isn't negative, this is refreshing entertaining content that shows that it's OK to fail and that it is humorous. The people that send us these videos are not ashamed they find it humorous. Now if you would like to submit your fails you can, but if you want to be negative then you need to leave my establishment! NOW!"...*

Alexis Dick Little's New Baby Boy--- *So I'm at the new and improved hospital in my hometown of Manhattan, Kansas aka Wild City, Kanziss. This hospital is bigger than I've ever seen it and so much nicer that it definitely accommodates for the growth Wild City has been experiencing over the years. As I'm at the entrance waiting room that's when I see and hear some of the nicest glass sliding doors I have ever seen open and an old friend of mines named Alexis Dick Little walks out with a newborn baby boy awake, small, and well aware of his surroundings in Alexis's arms. I'm not gonna lie, this was probably one of the cutest babies I have seen. This baby had a head full of hair and was so aware of his surroundings and Alexis is holding him like a proud father, as he should. I smiled at Alexis and I said to him "Congratulations my daw! Man he has a lot of hair!" And that's when Alexis gave me a weird look as if what I said was nonsense and he says to me "That's not a lot of hair!" That's when I laughed and replied back to him "For a baby? Uh yuh, your son has a full head of hair on his head already!" I meant that though, this kid had so much hair on his head he could have had a combover, bangs, blow out, etc. That's when Alexis's wife had come through the sliding doors and I then said "Well my daw I'm happy for you! Having kids is a beautiful thing especially your first child. Y'all are leaving already though after 2 days of being here?" As soon as I said that that's when Alexis and his wife had both scrunched their faces at me as a blonde little boy about 9 or so years old had stepped from behind Alexis Dick Little's wife and I got so confused because I swore this was Alexis's first and only kid being the baby in his arms, but I guess not! That's when they had slowly walked away from me towards the entrance/exit doors, all four of them, and myself feeling guilty because I think I may have offended them. That's when I yelled out "Having kids is a wonderful experience that's hard to explain, but it's magical!" As they continued out the hospital doors not even looking back or acknowledging me that's when all of a sudden I had…………………………………..*

Marlon's Craft & JID--- *So I'm walking from Bluemont Avenue to Anderson Avenue right by the MCC Campus which is the Manhattan Christian College here in my hometown of Manhattan, Kansas aka Wild City, Kanziss. Usually I'm either riding my bike or I'm dumbbell walking this path, but naw for some reason I'm just regular walking it today. As I'm walking I could hear some familiar music playing loudly behind me, but I can tell that it's not from a car or a nearby business, home, or apartment it's coming from some headphones. I turn around to see this young college White guy with a big ass stuffed book bag on his back and a big pair of plastic headphones that almost look like ear muffs. The song that's playing is by Marlon Craft "Here For It" which is a song that I like a lot by the Hell's Kitchen, New York rap artist. This fool has always gone so hard since I first heard him on cyphers on YouTube. Very talented and open minded unbiased White guy that is passionate about the art and science of hip hop. I stopped where I was at and the guy that was listening to Marlon Craft stopped and looked at me kind of scared as in "Did I do something wrong?" As he pulled his headphones off that's when I asked him "That's Marlon Craft right?" That's when he looks at me and says "Yeah." Kind of excited, but not sure what I was going to say to him next. That's when I then say "I like him. He goes hard. Always has from the amount of years I discovered him. What really blew him up and got him recognized was that song "Gang" and I remember being subscribed to him when he had 19,000 subscribers on YouTube and look at him now, over 103,000 subscribers now. Even before his "Gang" song he has been talking about institutionalized racism and the racism involved in this country and whatnot. He's a good artist that could make a change with his message and honesty." That's when that White guy nods his head in agreement and that's when I then asked him "Have you ever heard of the artist JID?".................................*

Offering Bed & GramInsta Report--- *So I've been invited over to a friends house that I met at one of my long time friends birthday party's not too long ago. The guy I met ended up being real cool and I found out he's been working at K-State for a few months now which was pretty ironic and funny because the same day I met him and he had told me he works for K-State was the same exact day I had applied for a job at K-State. Anyways, so I'm at this guy's place and I was seriously not expecting him to be living in an apartment building that was one room. I figured with his K-State pay that he would have had a nice home or at least a nicer apartment, but dizzamn that's what I get for assuming right? He has a small kitchen and an even smaller living room, a single room, but he shares a roommate that doesn't have a bed, but the bedroom is set up like a hotel room except it's missing another bed, and then there's a bathroom. I could just tell that with this setup there is literally no privacy. After the quick walkthrough which it seriously couldn't have gone any quicker than that that's when we go back to the bedroom and I'm standing where the roommates bed should be as I'm looking around the room thinking of ways I could help and that's when I said to the roommate "If you need a bed just let me know. I know where I can get you 2 mattresses and a box spring if needed." That's when the roommate responded with "Can that box spring fit on a window seal? Is it round?" I looked at this fool like "What the fuhh are you talking about?!" Then I could tell he read my facial expression which made him insecure and he kind of stepped back and that's when I then said "Naw. It's not rounded, but I can get you a box spring and 2 mattresses to set on top of so you don't need a bed frame if that's what you would like?" That's when he had looked at me nervously and I just decided to pull my phone out of my pocket after I just felt it vibrate and I got a notification from it* *from my GramInsta saying that a picture I had taken had been removed because it was considered inappropriate to GramInsta Terms and Conditions. I looked at the photo and I'm confused as fuhh because the picture that I had supposedly been reported for was not even a picture I had taken. The picture was of the guy that invited me over that I met at one of my friends' bday parties naked on his bed that is in this apartment which I have never been here before besides right now. He's on his knees on the bed with his legs spread as if he is trying to take a sexy photo. I never took this picture and I wouldn't take a picture of some shit like this so I don't know why or how it got in my phone. Now his roommate on the other hand has already proved to me that he can be a pretty weird White guy and he's nerdy and awkward and from this angle of this pic it definitely looks like whoever took this picture was from the angle of where myself and the White guy are at now. I don't know if my phone was connected to and hacked upon coming into this apartment, but the fact that I'm being reported for some shit that I did not post, would not post, or would have even been involved in makes me wonder how and who and why someone would do this to me and that's when I then say……………………………………*

K-Star & The White Rapper--- *So I'm in this lunch line sort of thing that has a salad bar and all you can eat buffet and all of that good stuff. I'm at the bar, the salad bar to be exact picking out food and what I plan to get with a couple of these dub dubs that apparently I have become good friends with as of recent. They're cool, friendly, and shexy and they have really good upbeat energy that vibrates off of them and I love it. As I'm coming from one end of the bar that's when I see this Black feezy that I use to work with looking at me very seriously as if I'm doing something wrong. I looked at her and I said "Aye! What's excellent?! How you been?" That's when she had just rolled her eyes and then said out loud with a bit of an attitude "I'm singing now! Got this White rapper too and him and I make some really good music!" That's when I responded with "That's good! Do y'all have any songs on YouTube I could listen to?" What program do y'all use?" That's when she had given an evil look to the White feezies I was with just eyeing them down until the White girls had walked away and they told me that they were going to our table and I said "Asiago. I'll meet y'all there in a little bit." Then that's when this White guy, tall, in a white tall tee had came out of nowhere and he put one of his arms around K-Star and smiled at me and K-Star had rolled her eyes at me and had walked away and the whole vibe I had gotten from here was that she was being resentful or holding some type of grudge against me that I have no idea about when I thought her and I were pretty cool………….*

A Tree & A Trailer--- *Here I am in this trailer park parking this old school white van we have to quickly see what the noise is that's going on under the hood of the van. It's my maintain and I. As I park the van on this hill like structure that's when I got out and I walked over to the front of the van until I noticed that with the gravity the braking wasn't going to be doing much as the van rolled over the hilly bump and the van was rolling towards a parked vehicle at this trailer and I panicked because I was afraid our van was going to run right into this old school oldsmobile as it was sliding towards it I wanted to run between them, but I was in so much shock and fear that I couldn't move I stayed stuck in anticipation of paying damages that my van will probably inflict on this old school Oldsmobile, but during the sliding of the van the van had turned to where only a panel in the front of the van had came loose and touched the Oldsmobile. My maintain still being in the van had given me this big eyed look of "That was fucking scary!" I walked to the* *van to get in and started it just to park it in a place that seemed safe, open, but yet shaded so I parked it 30 or so feet where we were at beside this big tree. As it's parked beside this tree I get out of the van again and this skinny older White woman comes out of her trailer waving at us as I did not notice this flat white old school metal car that was crushed at the top beside the tree on the other side of us. That older white lady steps in her grass and she looks up at the top of the tree with her hand above her eye brows blocking the sun and my maintain and I being curious as to what it is she's looking at or looking for we look up too and we notice how the top of the tree about 8 or so feet from the tip was sawed through. With just the right blow of the wind...The wind had blown and the branches and the other 8 feet of the tree had broken off and landed a couple of feet from the white old school car that looks like it has been smashed before. That was close! Then I looked down the tree and I noticed how the bottom portion of the tree has also been sawed down as well. It blows my mind how someone sawed this tree, but no one was around to supervise or to make sure the area was safe. Whoever did this has set this up to be very dangerous. As the wind picks up and you can see the swaying of the rest of the tall tree that's when everyone steps back not knowing which way this tree can fall whether that's on some vehicles, trailers, or some people. The wind picks up heavily and you could hear the snapping of the tree until it breaks off and it starts falling towards the trailer of that older White lady that had came outside and as the tree falls it looks so close to smashing that lady's trailer as we all gasp and stood back and the tree had just barely barely nicked the tin roof and the tree fell as we all let out a deep breath laughing and "whewwing" because we thought we were gonna witness a house demolition that was until...That woman's trailer had...collapsed and that's when we all looked at one another and back at her trailer as it was completely collapsed and folded in and everyone was speechless…………………………..*

<u>Inside The Home---</u> *So I'm inside of my trailer waking up from the living room couch and I don't know if it's late night or early morning, but there is no sun out and there are a lot of people in my home which is something that I'm not ever cool with especially people that I don't even know. I don't trust many people anyway. As everyone was running through the trailer I heard a knock on the door. As I get up from the couch and I see little kids running through the living room and hallways and adults moving through my home as I walk towards the front door very confused on who it could be, for who, and why and as I touched the door knob after unlocking the top and bottom lock and………………………….....*

<u>*Swimming To The Island---*</u> *So here I am at what seems to look like a San Francisco beach with my daw Big Joke and some young little White kid that looks as if he's about 13 or so years old. We're at the edge of the beach looking at this small little island about 40 or 50 feet from the edge of the beach. This island has that one little house on it that reminds me so much of Master Roshi's house on DragonBallZ which was one of my favorite shows growing up. As we are looking at this house that's when Big Joke says "I heard that they have some good stuff in there." That's when that little White boy and I looked at Big Joke with that "Yuh, what the fuck ever" look, but Big Joke looked serious as fuhh about what he had just said. That's when I say "I'm not much of a good swimmer my daw and my body doesn't float. A distance like that is further than I've ever gone. I'm not making up any excuses, but swimming is one way to get rid of me real quick." That's when Big Joke says "You won't drown. Just keep moving and I'll stay* *near you just in case. I'll make sure you don't go under." That's when I looked at that island saying out loud "I wonder if whoever stays there has a boat that brings their food and clothes? I wonder if they ever get lonely and bored? Does the waves or the sun ever bother them?" That's when Big Joke says "Only one way to find out!" As he jumps into the water and myself and that little White kid walk into the cold water a few seconds after Big Joke jumped in until the water gets about belly button deep and we began swimming as Big Joke was waiting on us as the waves were splashing us and as all 3 of us were side by side that's when we began swimming and that's when I noticed that I was swimming with my shoes on and that's when I yell out "Fuck! I kept my shoes on! This is gonna make it harder now!" That's when Big Joke says "You'll be good! Just swim and paddle harder! I got you!" As we were swimming and getting closer and closer to the island I realized that this wasn't bad at all. With each movement through the water we were getting closer and closer to this unique island and that's when…………………………*

Subliminal Messaging--- *Here I am waking up from the couch in my trailer's living room looking at the ceiling of a MADTV poster with that White guy's big ass face on it with this poster of these 2 dub dubs in a Jeep posted right below it. One brown hair and one blonde hair looking up as if they could be looking at the MADTV poster which is pretty funny to me. As I got up from the couch that's when I could hear a message go to my maintain's phone as I stood up and saw my maintain seated on the floor with her phone in her hand and I started walking past her to the kitchen and jokingly saying "Is that your boyfriend messaging you?" That's when she replied back with "No. It's Jasmine asking me if I would ever have some celebrity do this to me." As she turned her phone around to show me what was on her screen, but I wasn't tryna look at it at all. That just put me in a bad mood already as I walked over to the kitchen sink to start on some dishes and I just so happened to grab this pink glittery ashtray that had a top that you could snap on and off that had holes on it. It was nice that she made this, like really nice. I began washing it, but as I began washing it I got to thinking about what my maintain's friend had sent her and how my maintain should have said "Naw. I'll have Bryan do that to me." But she didn't. Then I got to thinking about why SHE has an ashtray for herself when she had stopped smoking when she was pregnant with our son. Everything started swirling around in my mind until I just fucking yelled and I threw the ash tray and broke it once it had hit the wall and I looked at my maintain and I yelled out "YOU SHOULD FUCKIN' TOLD YOUR FRIEND THAT YOU ONLY THINK ABOUT DOING THINGS WITH ME! SO FUCK YOU! AND FUCK HER!" As I turned around to look out the kitchen window to see the bright sun then I saw one of the fools I grew up with that's suppose to be in Colorado Springs walking, well sneaking into the back door of my neighbors trailer and I thought that was pretty weird and wondered what the fuck they had going on there and that's when………………………….....*

Look At My Jeans!--- *So I'm onset of this new rap video with these up and coming rap artists called "The Nap Crew" and their hit song called "Look At My Jeans." What's unique about this song is that they are not only talking about name brand and expensive jeans, but they are talking about the pairs of jeans they work hard in and also metaphors for "jeans" and "genes" as in genetics in their 3rd and final verse. Has rap changed? Yuh it has! But what I love about this crew is how they check their beat selection very wisely with what sounds good in a car and* *in the club, but they never ever dumb their lyrics down. Each individual artist builds one another and compliments one another so well that it's hard to say who the best rapper in the crew is. The bass is knocking and the chorus is "Look At My Jeans" as the crew does a dance as they say it and the bass knocks for a couple of seconds then the crew says "Look At My Jeans" then the bass knocks. Not only does The Nap Crew have a great beat selection and great lyrics they are putting together a great album and they also are trendsetters with songs and dances that put so much more fun in the music. As we are all onset with this phenomenal crew, that's when everyone, even the camera crew, was dancing and moving side to side and…………………..*

Inventing A Healthy Soda--- *So here my maintain and I are in our home made laboratory where we have been working on a healthy soda that is very flavorful, but yet so beneficial that people can't help, but to be addicted to. We know that most people will choose soda over natural drinks or whatever so we have been working on a drink so good that it's good for you! Our plan is to put this drink into an aluminum can that is taller than most that holds so much flavor and is so healthy and every can has an appealing cover on it with a code on the bottom of the can for promo's and great deals. My maintain and I are super excited to go into business together and build an empire for even more generational wealth. We are in our lab coats with formulas written all over the place with fruits and sweeteners everywhere. We have multiple flavors, but we are looking for that perfect new one as we begin to put a formula together that contains……………………*

K-18 & That White Truck--- *Here I am on K-18 driving my white Chevy Impala coming by the airport on my way to my sisters house on the way towards Junction City. As I'm driving and just relaxing by myself enjoying some time out of town to see new things and get new thoughts, insights, and aspirations that's when I heard a truck just revving up fast as fuhh coming up by me. Usually these big truck fools always rev their engines seeking some kind of attention especially when I'm outdoors working out with my dumbbells. I usually don't pay them any mind, but this truck was desperately trying to get my attention as they kept revving their engine beside me I looked over to see this big ass white truck and this country ass looking White fool looking as if he was cussing me out until I saw that was blatantly what he was doing when he had flipped me off and I instantly noticed who the fuck this fool was. Earlier this day after leaving the Chinese restaurant this fool waited for my family and I to walk to our van and as soon as all of us were behind him he revved out of his parking spot when even my 3 year old son was behind the truck which it pissed me off and I started cussing this fool out, but he was staying in his truck and rolling off talking shit, but only burned out and drove away after flipping me off and never getting out of his truck. So here we are again side by side on the highway going over 60 miles an hour coming towards the airport as we are speeding up going to 70s trying to pass one another as I'm in the right lane and he's in the left and that's when I see 2 trucks ahead of me one black and one white get over in the left lane because a cop had pulled someone over on the far right and the white truck beside me is staying right next to me not allowing me to get over so as I'm still going over 70 miles per hour I zoom right past the cop car and the car that's pulled over and I know that this could result in a ticket and I'm having an anxiety attack by constantly looking in my rearview mirror waiting for that cop to come chasing* *after me at any moment now as all the trucks near me in the left lane are all speeding at least in the 80s now and that's when……………………………………*

AirPort Only Fans--- *So here I am at this big city airport with my maintain with me as I pass out flyers to promote my OnlyFans account which might look ridiculous to some, but I'm an opportunistic person. It's bright and big windows are everywhere and the heat feels good on us. As people are coming through the hallway and we are moving towards them that's when I see these 2 very attractive dub dub stewardesses very tall and model looking. One brunette and one blonde with both of them having blue eyes and already tall, but the high heels make them taller and even more slender and shexy. These feezies should definitely be some runway models. They are eyeing me down as if I am more attractive than they are which I appreciate the eye compliment, but dizzamn they are frazy if they think that! They look good as fuhh! As we all walk closer and closer towards one another and the shexual tension is being felt at a higher vibration I could feel my maintain feeling uneasy about something, but as the stewardesses approach us they stop right in front of me standing tall and very attractive I hand my flyers to them for my OnlyFans as they read it and got super excited and that's when they had put their hands out to touch and rub all over me and then go in for a hug and that's when……………………………...*

Late Train Chicago--- *I'm in this motel room with my maintain and my momster in law spazzing out because I don't know how or when, but I lost track of time to get on my train to Chicago. I'm looking at my ticket print off where it says train pick up at 6am, but then I look at my cell phone and it showed a time of 5:49am and that's when my eyes got all big and I yelled out "Fuck!" As my maintain and her mom look at me and I'm thinking about if I have enough time to get to the AmTrak Topeka station from where we are at right now. I step out of the motel room and upon stepping out into the bright and cold morning day that's when I saw these 2 older Black guys outside of their motel room as we are on the 2nd floor balcony and they both have on these heavy looking black leather coats and these black skull caps as they looked at me and gave me the head nod signaling "What's up?" As I gave them a head nod back as they put their cigarettes to their mouths and…………………………..*

Slam Dunk Gym--- *Here I am after a year off from stepping into an actual gym since the whole closing of the world and the pandemic occurred. Ever since the gym has been closed I have been super determined and motivated to do my workouts outside everyday no matter the weather patterns and not letting anything or anyone stop me because health, weath, and myself is important and I should always be in control of all 3. I'm stepping into the new gym that is the same brand, but newly remodeled and new location and bigger, but this looks like a city gym. Once I walked in I saw new equipment and great things in here. It looks clean, big, and nice! I am completely impressed with the inside of this gym just as much as I am with the outside appearance. I walk onto the floor and I see a lot of people working out and a lot of people looking at me. Some people are looking at me because they recognize me as "The DumbBell Guy" and some because they were wondering when I was going to come back and whatnot. A year off from the gym and doing nothing, but outdoor workouts and home workouts and I'm back in the gym stronger and bigger than before. I'm too determined to let anything or anyone ever* *stop me and my prime example is that I'm always in my prime being actual proof. I'm walking past people and I'm looking around at the new equipment as I'm not going to be in the gym as many days of the week that I was before and that I'm going to scope out certain equipment for exercises I have been lacking in such as machines for my back and legs. As I'm walking past everyone staring at me I'm looking around and I see this equipment that I'm astonished by and absolutely surprised they have which is this replica of the "Slam Dunk" obstacle course I had seen on American Ninja Warrior that looked like it went so hard on. I walked up to it and a group of people with my daw Rickardo had stepped out of nowhere and they stood next to me as they wanted to not only see me try this machine out, but they were anxious to try it as well. I analyzed the machine and remembered how the contestants on American Ninja Warrior had to maneuver it and what the contestants said and even the hosts and I envisioned how I was going to do so. I walked over to the start off point of this obstacle course and I began stretching while staring at each slam dunk ball. I wiped my hands off on my sweatpants in preparation of this course and I jumped up and grabbed the handles of the first ball and started swinging my body and thought about how much core and upper body strength was needed for this type of challenge and as I began picking up momentum swinging back and forth that's when I had thrown my body and the ball into the next hole and the placement worked out as I had shifted over to the next part of the obstacle course. I am being applauded by the people watching and I'm focusing on swaying my body back and forth once again picking up momentum as I look at the next ball I have to transfer to that is higher up. As I continuously move back and forth that's when I let go of the handles of my slam dunk ball and I transferred over to the next ball, but not realizing how not only was the next balls platform was higher, but the ceiling was not too far from it so in the process of transferring over I had jammed my fingers into the ceiling which had shifted my balance and I began to fall to the ground. As everything had gone slow-mo and I could hear everyone's gasps. When I had landed on my feet awkwardly with a weird stance before I had regained my balance that's when one of the skinny guys from Rickardo's crew had already began on the obstacle course and I'm staring at the obstacle course where I had failed at and I'm beating myself up inside about how I almost had it and how close I was and…………..*

The Shitty Bus--- *Here we are, my maintain and I in this big, but yet so abused and beaten up city on this rainy and gloomy looking day. Like, this city is big! But the part of town that we are at is sad looking as you can just tell that this side of the city has been through a lot of adversity that has not recovered or been the same to this day. This city has a lot of history and as we are just cruising through scoping out as much as we can because we don't know when the next time we will get a vacation or time off to do so again and because we like to make the best out of our time out of town and our vacations. As we are at a stop light that's when we see this big grey metal city bus just speed right past us plowing through the wind and the rain as if those 2 things don't exist and as if hydroplaning doesn't exist as well and my maintain and I looked at one another with that "What, the, fuhh?!?!" face and we………………………..*

Library Levels--- *Here I am in this nice library that stands about 4 stories or so tall. Nice big city library and I'm on the 4th story that has a library section with shelves and books of course, but once you get to the end of the wall on this side of the library room there is a wooden door with a glass window that you can go through that will take you to another side of the library with* *even more books and great selections. As I'm going through the books I get this weird vibe that something bad is about to happen. That's when I realized that I was a character in a video game and on my screen I am told to crouch down and to act like I'm looking for a specific book as this one Black guy in this black leather motorcycle jacket cannot get too far past me when he comes in my direction. As I'm pretending that I'm looking for a specific book, that's when the black leather motorcycle jacket guy moves as if he was tipped off that whatever or whoever he was looking for is nearby. He keeps his head in the direction that I'm in then he starts walking my direction. As I'm still fake searching for a book that's when the instructions on my screen now said "Protect the rapper Mack Drazzle from the assassination attempt!" That's when the game consoles controller started vibrating and shaking as the black leather motorcycle jacket guy steps in closer and closer and as he passes me that's when I slowly stood up and followed behind me, but not too close because I didn't want my reflection to be seen in that wooden doors window. He goes through that door so I followed behind him and as he goes through the door the video game goes to a story part where that black leather motorcycle jacket guy had spotted Mack Drazzle upon opening the door to the other side and pulling Mack Drazzle's 9mm from his waist line while Mack Drazzle tries to grab it from the motorcycle jacket guy, but the motorcycle guy was quick and seemed highly trained and already had the gun off of safety and aimed at Mac Drazzle's forehead and that's when he shot the rapper and everyone had scattered throughout the library and screams are being heard from all around the building….Then here I go again starting off in the same part of the library where I had to crouch down to fake look for a book on this bookshelf and here comes this White feezy zooming through this library floor on an actual motorcycle and stopping all the way on the other end of this top floor by the big glass windows. The instructions on my screen had said "Go through the wooden and glass door and try not to be overly noticed." That's when I had stood up with a book in my hand and I walked towards the door to the other side of the library as I could see this White feezy in a pink, light beige, and white leather motorcycle outfit watch me go through the doors. As I went through the door that's when that White feezy started power walking towards the doors I had gone through and now my instructions on the screen said "Hurry and go near the crowd of people on the other end of this room and get completely on the floor!" So I ran past the bookshelves and I slid on the floor as the console controller was shaking and pulsating as this game was definitely made to give anxiety attacks and to get you so involved into the game, but you can see why it's so addicting and why so many love it. So as I'm on the ground and looking through the books and the shelves that's when my characters nervousness had began kicking in and I began throwing up chunks on the floor and that's when the crowd of people began making noises in disgust and started to walk away and as that motorcycle lady came further into the room I could see her looking over in this direction. As I slowly get up to a crouching position and I began walking away and towards the check out desk while holding my throw up in to keep quiet that's when I walked over to the check out desk as the motorcycle lady was walking over towards the direction I had left a pile of throw up and as I'm about to throw up again that's when I wake up from this video game dreams with a little bit of throw up coming out of my mouth and onto my actual pillow before I had flipped my pillow over to go back to sleep and…………………………………..*

Wal-Mart Rack Restrooms--- *So my maintain and I are at the Wal-Mart in our hometown of Manhattan, Kansas aka Wild City, Kanziss in the clothes aisle as my maintain is looking for some new jeans and shirts. As we are looking around I noticed how there are so many more people than usual shopping around and the store is crowded and usually when a store is this crowded it means that some event especially a football game is what's happening. As I'm looking on the rack for shirts I think my maintain would look good in or that she would like that's when I looked over at her and she has this "Uh Oh!" face on and she's just standing still with her eyes all big. I ask her "What's wrong?!" That's when she says "I gotta shit!" That's when I started lightly laughing, but then you could tell that this was a serious matter so I began looking around and that's when I noticed that in each of these shirt racks there were restrooms in the middle of them. I tell my maintain "Go through the shirts and go in there." That's when she gives me this look then says "No! There's people all around here looking for shirts! They're gonna hear me and smell me. Plus there's someone in that one right now." That's when I then said "Can you hear whoever is in there or smell them? They're gonna hear, see, and smell you if you shit yourself!" That's when she looks at me and gives me that "Touche! You did just make a good point just now" look. That's when I then told her "I'll look for an empty one and I'll go in it just so you feel comfortable about them." So as I walked away from the shirt rack we were at as I slowly and carefully walked by a couple more shirt racks looking over the top to check the small port-a-potty type restrooms in the middle for occupied or not that's when I saw that no one is in the one that's 3 racks away. I crouched down to get on the shirts level and I spread open a walk through of the shirts and as I stepped through towards the restroom that's when…………………………*

Outdoor Exercises, P.R.'s, And--- *So here I am outdoors at the tennis racket court for some reason in the city park of Wild City, Kanziss. It's myself, my oldest sister, a bunch of mutual friends, an older crowd, my daw Goolian and his dad. We are all doing leg raises for now as we are to keep our feet and heels above the ground for as long as we can for not only our personal records, but to set the tone for others to beat as well. My sister and I are next to one another and we are watching one anothers legs making sure they don't touch and that's when she starts saying "Your legs touched! Your feet and heels touched!" But she's saying it in a straining voice and that's when her heels had touched the ground and as I'm still in my position and holding my feet up that's when I could hear something hitting the ground, but in a skipping pattern as I turned my head the direction of the sound and it's Goolian's late 60's something years old dad jump roping fluently and he makes it look so blissful and effortless fun as the skin on his neck sags and moves, but for him to be so active and smooth with it at his age goes to show his health, his mindset, his goals, experiences, etc. As we continued to watch him, that's when he began to………………………………………......*

A Thomp & I Talk--- *So here we are. My long time schoolmate from elementary through high school A. Thomp and I at the gym that I go to sitting down at a gym sales table talking about the growth of our hometown Wild City, Kanziss, the gym, and exercise. He has known me since I was a little short kid obsessed with fighting and DragonBallz. Here I am today being such a motivational guy and influencer not only in my town, but over the internet as well. Why are me and A. Thomp seated at this gym table at this point in time now? Well, it's because we want to* *learn and grow from one another and that's something that we are going to do as we talk about fitness and technology and gaining insights, knowledge, and wisdom from one another and working on our personal goals as one and making a super team that could definitely bring change and everlasting powerful results. In exchange for personal training that I will be giving A. Thomp, he will be teaching me more about technology, computers, and building a website. Once we intertwine the two and show both of our results and myself being able to sell my product which is my time with personal training, my clothing apparel, my books, and my music not only will my income be diversified, but my clients will be as well and I would be able to reach so many people that this is going to be bigger than Wild City, Kanziss alone. As A. Thomp and I are drawing up a business plan and jotting down ideas I can't stop, but keep thinking about this great expansion and how incredible and exciting this is going to be once this great plan is executed outside of this building. As I'm coming up with ideas and A. Thomp is coming up with ideas that's when we had decided to go with………………………………………*

Lil' Skies Studio Session--- *Here I am! Wild City, Kanziss late night on Juliette Avenue right next to Bluemont Elementary. I've been out and about riding my bike to get some fresh air and some new thoughts and inspiration by seeing new and more things differently from a late night bike ride other than a car ride. I've been so active and busy with promoting my name and my brand that now I'm to the point of getting back into the music and applying everything I have learned along the way to prove to the world what relentlessness does for you. I have been studying rap so fluently and aggressively that I have even shocked myself at times with the rhyme patterns and creativity I have come up with and have even written down. I am a YOUnique individual! So someway somehow I have rap artist Lil' Skies number and although it's about 9 or 10p.m. I feel so confident to meet with this fool in a studio to record a song or few with him and feel so strongly about it that I know our songs can be hits and or classics. As I am on the sidewalk close to the playground fence to the elementary school that's when I leaned up against the fence to pull out my phone and got to my contacts to look for Lil' Skies number as I found it and I pressed the green phone icon to call him as I put my phone to my ear to hear the phone ring until it was picked up on the other line and I told Lil' Skies "Let's meet up at the studio my daw. I'm ready…………………………………………...*

Laughed & Boo'd--- *So there's this Black comedian I have seen on stage several times before named D. Lemon. This guy is hilarious! Just about everything he says and the way he says it is unique. He's on stage talking about White women for his bit and how Black men react to White women and how funny they are. He then gets to talking about how every Black man needs to get him a White woman and some guys are clapping, but only some are. The rest are either quiet or they're at the show with their Black girlfriend or wife. As Lemon goes on about why, that's when the crowd starts booing and they're taking so much offense to what he is joking about when this is some hilarious stuff. He's not joking about the same old stereotypes most people say about high credit scores, being pulled over, etc. He's talking about giving dick to White women so deep that it changed their ancestors thinking of Blacks. He's talking about digging into White women so deep that their ancestors turned in their grave to get the dick in their ass too! He also says things about how Black men and White women make racial tension a 50/50 hate, love situation literally. This stuff to me is hilarious, but this majority Black crowd* *was not trying to listen to not only his comedy and his jokes, but they didn't want to hear the truth in it as well. In my opinion Lemon's jokes and stage performance was great, but it was just tonight's crowd that he was working for. I understand that racial tension on the news has been displayed ridiculously, but it's these stressful current events that should not only be talked about, but made to make others aware of the problems and not ignored, but to be able to know what's going on, but feeling a bit of escape by being able to find humor and laugh at the ones that think they're doing good in the situation that only make things worse. Laugh at the cops, laugh at the racists, it's the insecure White men that feel like they can abuse power and rights of others, but it's White women that are on mutual grounds that are and can be on both sides to either diffuse or make things worse. Lemon is one of the funniest guys with original content, but this crowd right here does not like this bit that he's doing. I'm sure he's going to work the crowd and get them to laughing soon though, that was until……………………………..*

The Parking Garage--- *So here we are! My friend Scarie and I are on the 3rd level of this big hotel parking garage walking up the road as we are catching up on the things we have both been dealing with in life. We don't see each other as much, but whenever she is in town we seem to always have somewhat of a good time although she does talk so much! We stopped walking when we found this one spot that seemed comfortable. As we are standing and talking that's when this tall Black fool I know named Ant 1 comes out of nowhere just looking at us and just stands for a while as he turns around with his back facing us. Scarie and I are still talking, but looking at Ant 1 and Scarie and I are giving one another looks like "What the fuhh?!" Ant 1 then sits down on the concrete and he's facing our way, but not looking at us. It's almost as if he is either listening to our conversation or is wanting to ask us something. As Scarie is still talking I'm looking around for another location her and I could possibly go to talk and also a place that would have some great camera angles and lighting for my videos and that's when I could see the perfect place on the next level of the parking garage so that's when we……………...*

Deep Paralysis In A Sleep Sleep--- *After waking up as I usually do early in the morning at 3:30a.m. I am extremely tired today as I have been feeling it throughout the week, but kept falling asleep during my writing. As I write and type my dreams and get up to help my maintain get ready to go to work and get our youngest son together I have been debating on whether I want to go back to bed or not and to call in or go to work. My maintain tells me to go to sleep after calling in, but I'm still thinking about all of the things that I need to do. After putting my son in the van with my maintain I go back inside and I decide to call my jobs call in line and extension to leave a voicemail. I quickly put my phone on airplane mode and laid down on my bed to go to sleep and let my body get the rest that it deserves. After falling into a deep sleep that's when I heard dishes fall into my kitchen sink next to my bedroom very loudly. It scared me because I'm the only one in the trailer right now and that makes me feel like someone or something is in the trailer with me that's not supposed to be. I try to get up from the bed and open my eyes, but I'm not able to do either one. I can't move my arms or my legs or open my eyes and I'm just under a blanket, scared, and in darkness. I'm seeing things in the darkness, but it's like even though I can't open my eyes I can see myself standing up in darkness while in front of me things are making shapes with lights then a hooded boney figure with razor sharp* *teeth looks at me smiling standing in front of me as if it is intimidating me and that's when I try to move my arms and legs still and I yell out to the hooded figure "FUCK YOU FAG!! FUCK YOU!!!" As loud as I could and my arms and legs moved and that's when I woke up from my sleep and I lifted up to see sunlight through the blinds in the room and I get up from my bed to go to the kitchen and dishes are in the sink, but not all over the place, they are still stacked as if they never fell. I grabbed a cinnamon roll and went to the living room to sit on the couch and eat it and try to stay up to get a head start on things since I called in today. After eating my cinnamon roll I am still tired, but nervous to go back to sleep over such a vivid dream I had just had and not being able to move my body and being in this trailer by myself. I get up from the couch and throw the plastic wrapper for the cinnamon roll away in the kitchen trash can and I go back into the bedroom with plans of laying down because my mind and body is still exhausted and that's when I laid back down and…………………...*

Inn The Hot Blonde--- *Here I am at this hotel with a whole bunch of feezies and myself being like the only fool with all of these feezies. We are leaving out of the hotel elevator laughing and all over one another going down to the lobby and even my maintain is with us. After a while I find out that these are my entourage groupies that go wherever I go and do whatever I want and we all have fun with one another. Everywhere we go and everything we do has a strong presence and we build a fan base organically so fast because people see the positivity and the fun and they want to know what it is we do and how to be a part of it or support what we have going on. We are walking through the lobby talking loudly and laughing, but no one is complaining as we are exiting the hotel to the parking lot to get into this small ass car and pack in it as we are getting ready to do something new. We all packed into this small ass aqua green Honda squeezed in tightly, but this one blonde feezy has been looking at me in such a shexual way and rubbing all over me to the point where we are about to fuck in the car with everyone around us, but we decided to get out of the car and tell everyone "We will be back! We gotta get something and do something right quick!" Everyone in the car looks at us with that "OK. Whatever then!" look as we got out and power walked then ran back into the hotel lobby and straight to the elevator. As the both of us got into the elevator and before the doors would completely close that blonde dub dub and I were already on one another kissing and touching so much that I could feel how wet she was through her jeans and my dick left a bulge so out there that I swear it was going to rip through my pants. The elevator goes up to Floor 3 and we rushed out of the elevator back towards our room we had as she's sucking on my neck and rubbing my dick while she has her hands in my pants and I pulled out the room key card to open the door and we barged through the door as this blonde dub dub pulls my dick out of my pants and says "Come on! Fuck me!" As she runs over to the bed closest to the door and jumps on the bed landing on her back and then taking her clothes off of her so fast and throwing them onto the floor exposing her whole nice looking tight body. Small frame, legs open with her pretty pink pussy and some tight lips, nice flat stomach, perky tits with pink nipples, bright blue eyes, and long blonde hair. My dick was harder than ever as I took my clothes off thinking to myself how I'mma fuhh the shhh out of somebody's daughter. I got on the bed as she spreads her legs even wider and I'm between them on top of her and that's when she puts her arms up and puts her arms and hands on my shoulders as she's preparing to take my long hard dick inside of her. She looks down and she looks at my dick and she says "Oh my GOSH! That thing is big! Like* *really big! Wow! OK! Put it in! PUT IT IN! FUCK M…" before she could even finish her demand that's when I slid my dick inside of her tight wet pussy and she let out a deep breath and I started stroking her quickly and she was getting wetter and wetter and I was going deeper and deeper and harder and harder as she began moaning uncontrollably and was pulling my body in closer to hers and she started scratching my back and I could feel her wetness rolling down my balls as they dangled and was slapping underneath her pussy as I was rocking the bed and fucking her so good as I can tell she has never been fucked like this before. As we are so into the moment and I'm kissing her and she's moaning and screaming that's when we both heard the door to the hotel room shut and I automatically thought my maintain had walked in on me smashing another feezy which I got scared and my heart started pumping even harder, but I didn't stop stroking my dick in this blonde dub dub because I figured I might as well go out with a bang if this is how I'm gonna get caught cheating as I looked over at the direction our room door was, but I didn't see anyone so as I'm still fucking the dub dub I look over to the other side of the room and it was a brunette White feezy with her arms crossed as she's just looking at us almost disappointed because she's not involved in what we are doing. The dub dub that I'm so deep in is still moaning as I'm still thrusting and pounding her is looking at the brunette as if she was caught doing something she wasn't supposed to, but she's still holding onto me tightly and wanting me to fuck her still even though I could feel that she's drying up and not as wet as she was before we had heard the door close. As I'm still fucking the blonde dub dub and the brunette is watching us I was bout to ask her if she wanted to join that was until we heard the door to our room open and close again and the dub dub I'm smashing is drying up even more, but still wants me to smash her and here comes this black haired White guy that's now standing on the end of the bed watching me smash this dub dub and he has his arms folded and watching just like the brunette feezy to my right and from where the guy is at he has an angle on my balls hitting the dub dubs ass hole. At this point I just want to bust my nut because I don't know who the fuck this guy is at least and I don't know what they want or who's going to come into the room next especially thinking about if my maintain catches us in the act and that's when I tell the dub dub I'm smashing to get ready to bend over because I want to hit it from the back and clap it hard and fast and bust a nut all over her back, but that's when…....I woke up from my actual sleep with my dick hard so I J.O.'d and went back to sleep after imagining how it would have felt and ended with that dub dub and……………………*

Ball Park--- *Here I am on the porch of my in-laws at the trailer park with my maintain, our oldest son, and the monster in law. It's a nice warm summer day and we are enjoying the outdoors and the summer, finally. My maintain had stepped inside with our oldest because he said he wanted his mom to make him some cinnamon rolls. My momster in law gives me this shexual seductive look from my shoes up and she holds her eyes in the area of my dick and my dick got hard as fuhh! I didn't even try to hide it, I didn't care because obviously the way she looked at me let me know that she not only wanted to see my dick, but she wanted to feel it too, inside of her. As my dick was getting harder and harder and the temptation was getting stronger that's when my momster in law looked up from my dick area to my stomach to my chest and my face and that's when she gave me this look of seduction as she licked her lips and that's when I stood up from my chair on the porch and I walked over towards her and I………………*

Rejection From A Knock Out To A Knock Out--- *I'm in the movie theatre parking lot, the old movie theatre in my hometown that we all miss and took for granted when it was active over by the trailer park RedBud in my hometown of Manhattan, Kansas aka Wild City, Kanziss. It's sunny and bright and as I'm stepping out of my car to walk towards the movie theatre that's when I see this white car with this White feezy in the passenger seat by herself. From where I see her she looks good as fuhh, brown hair, small body, shexy ass face with a little bit of an attitude on it, but it's all shexy to me. I step away from my car towards this distraction attraction of a feezy and I walk up to her car and that's when I noticed she wasn't in the car by herself. There was a blonde dub dub in the driver's seat. From the angle I was at I didn't see her until now. She looks good as fuhh too, but my mind was already made up with the feezy with the brown hair. I figured they were friends and I could hang out with both of them and see what movie they were planning to see. As I stepped up to the white car that's when I head nodded the brown haired feezy and I stepped in close on the driver's side and waved at her and hunched down and I said "What's your name?" That's when the blonde dub dub looked over at the brown haired feezy and the brown haired feezy said to me "Naw. I'm good." Then the blonde dub dub looked at me and laughed and I was like "OK. I was just gonna say….." Then the brown haired feezy said "I'm good. Go watch your movie!" I was like "Dizzamn!" I was gonna talk to the blonde dub dub, but then I figured that they were either dating each other, dating someone else, or that they didn't like Black guys or just me. I walked away and into the movie theatre wondering what it was about me that they had no interest in at all. "Was it my breath? My approach? My physique? What could it be?" I was mind boggled and so confused! As I stepped into the movie theatre that's when I could see one of the fools I grew up with eyeing me down aggressively when I thought that him and I were cool until now. He walks up to me aggressively and says "You talking to the bitch out there with the brown hair with fucked up teeth?" Which I completely forgot about her teeth which I did notice, but forgot simply because I was thrown off by the rejection and not even wanting to know what I was going to say or give her a compliment in. I have never been rejected like that ever before! That's when I looked at this fool that asked me that and I said "Yuh. I tried to why?" That's when his face scrunched up and he yelled back "You nasty mawfucka! YOU….." before he could finish his disrespectful sentence I felt a surge of aggression and adrenaline flow through my body and I automatically hit this fool so hard that the contact echo'd so hard knocking him the fuck out so hard that I could feel his bones crack and his body drop lifelessly to the ground and I looked at Crab Bucket for a few seconds making sure he was still breathing which he was and that's when I turned around to see both of those feezies that were in the white car in the movie theatre parking lot behind me holding hands looking at me and then Crab Bucket knocked out on the floor and that's when they…………………………..*

My Maintain Coming In The Back Door--- *Here I am sleeping, well waking up from my sleep because I'm hearing something at the backdoor of my trailer trying to get in. At first I thought it was the washing machine or dryer, but then again I remembered how all the laundry is caught up. I jumped up from the bed and I ran towards the backdoor where the noise was from especially since I'm the only one in the trailer because I stayed home from work for being so tired. As I'm looking at the back door I see it and hear it being beaten in and then a powerful* *kick at the door had me paranoid so I ran to the door and pushed my weight against it and, but the door was already kicked in as I'm trying to keep the person from coming in and that's when I could see and hear that it's my maintain mad as fuhh with a knife in her hand yelling out some shit and that's when I………………………………*

A H.E. (A Humbling EXperience)--- *Here I am in this big house, this big 2 story house, well if you count the basement and the attic we have 4 stories. Lots of people are in this house as if we had or are about to have an adult sleepover or swinger party, but I'm noticing how most of the people in here are women. It's late night now and my maintain and I were on the couch until my maintain had fallen asleep, but I'm still full of energy and not ready to fall asleep. I'm curious to see what else is going on and who else is in the house. I slowly get up from the couch without waking my maintain up. I stood up from the couch slowly and I looked at my maintain for a few seconds to make sure she was still sleeping and snoring, which she was. I slowly crept out of the living room and into the hallway past rooms where I had seen other people in. No one or nothing of my interest had popped out as there are some people fucking, but they look neshty to me so I'm not going to watch or join. People of all ages are throughout this house from 18 to old as fuhh! But they like to fuck! I'm assuming that my maintain had only agreed to come here because of me because she's not big into fucking like I am and I'm sure she had also come here to make sure no one would try to fuck me or flirt with me. I'm walking through the house more and more and seeing some frazy shexual shit from dominatrix, straps, pegging, threesomes, cuckolds, lesmerizing lesbians, interracial, etc. This is some frazy shit and almost neshty only because it's something I'm not involved in, but I think that anything I was involved in with any feezy would be so much fun. As I continue to walk through the house until I find something of interest or to record that's when I came across a second living room/guest room that had another bed in it and this bed is nice! King size or maybe a California King so big, tall, and fluffy with like 4 or 5 adults on it. One feezy that stood out was this blonde feezy that looked super familiar to the point where I had to triple to almost quadruple check and yuh it was who I thought it was, my ex ShaNaNa looking at me as she is on the end of the bed. She lifts her head up a little bit as I walk into the room towards her and I rub on her as if I know or I want to fuck her after seeing her already. I slowly got into the bed with her although this bed has so many people in it already and I got comfortable and I slowly started rubbing on her, but I felt a different type of energy from her that I have never felt before. Usually or ALL THE TIME she is on me and ready to fuck, but not this time. As I was about to get more aggressive and lean up from the bed to make out with her as I put my hand in her pants and that's when my maintain had slowly walked into the room and that's when ShaNaNa stood up from the bed and says to me "You can't stay committed to one woman or have respect for a woman because of your relationship with your mom growing up. No woman deserves that and you need to find that peace with women or else you're going to go through life hurting women because the woman that was supposed to love you has done and said some hurtful things to you. YOU NEED to learn to let those things go because you have been the same Bryan since I met you in high school. It's time to let go of that because you are successful, but you are not happy because your childhood and your mom bothers you! You want to be happy right? With the person you are with right?" That's when my maintain stepped in closer with tears and hurt in her eyes and I felt so bad because everything ShaNaNa had said was trueness as fuhh! Those words had cut* *me deep and I couldn't help, but respect it and dwell on it because I knew it was the truth about me that is so hard for me to get over or to effectively cope with. Here are 2 women I have hurt and I continue to have people hold resentment against me because of my childhood pain that I have continued into my adulthood and…………………………………...*

<u>After The Pyramids---</u> *After a trip to the pyramids in Egypt and seeing some very unique and historical things we are on the road back to our hotel to change our clothes, relax for a little bit, and hydrate before we go to our next tourist attraction. It's amazing with just the thought alone of being here and seeing some of the oldest structures by the earliest people in our human history that we know of. I wonder what the evolution was like over time. How different we look compared to people centuries ago. The thought, creativity, and ideas coming to my head that is so unique and inspirational that I'm becoming more and more open minded the more that I'm seeing and being around these things and places that I would not normally see in the United States or my hometown of Manhattan, Kansas aka Wild City, Kanziss at all. As we are all in this Jeepish like vehicle all 4 of us, we notice someone speeding up behind us so aggressively and fast to the point where they are only about 3 feet or so behind our bumper and I look in the rearview and it's a fucking mummy in a vehicle behind us ready to kill us. This was no prank at all as sand was coming up behind the mummy's car and bugs, frogs, locusts, hieroglyphs, etc. could be seen and as I picked up the speed of our Jeepish looking vehicle that's when we had been in the complete bright sunlight to now literally about to enter darkness with stars right in front of us about 20 feet away and that's when I was debating on slamming the breaks and getting hit by the mummy behind us, to swerve off of the road and have everything the mummy was bringing with him catch us, or to drive straight into what seemed to be space on earth and that's when…………………………………..*

<u>Dirty Love---</u> *Here I am on this huge farm that's so peaceful, blissful, open, and relaxing. This seems like such a movie that I'm in or on set of. There's this blonde young country feezy on the field sitting on her lawn chair in the sun fully dressed just thinking about her life and what she wants to do after an argument her and her boyfriend had gotten into the night before over her wondering or debating on moving to the big city to pursue a career and to leave the country and be able to support herself. As her man is covered in dirt and sweat on this automatic tiller that's so high tech that it's almost like a scooter type with the standing position and riding it with the controls and throttle and clutch. As he's pulling up the dirt and making it looser that's when he pulls up to his blonde deep thinking maintain and stops the tiller a few feet from her so no dirt is flung up on her and he turns the tiller off and walks up to her and he's been sweating so much and with dirt flung on him he basically looks as if he was rolling in mud more than anything. He walks up to his maintain and as she wants to look at him, but is forcing herself not to, that's when he says with such a country accent "I love you girl! I just want you to know that I'm sorry and hurt at the same time. I can't see myself with anyone but you. I hope that we can come to a mutual agreement for us to stay together. In the meantime though….WILL YOU MARRY ME?!" As he gets down in the dirt on both knees covered in dirt, but so meaningful with his action and words and that's when his maintain could not help, but look at him and the ring as she was blushing so hard that her whole face had turned red and it made her blue eyes stand* *out so strongly as she busted out into tears and reached out to the ring with her red fingernail polished fingernails and that's when………………………..*

Weight Lost Body Destruction Tournament--- *After months of preparation my older daw Jafay has told me that he feels comfortable enough to jump back on stage to do his bodybuilding shows and a comeback for nearly 10 years of being absent. I have not seen him in months because he has said he is going into hiding and dedicating his time to have the best body ever in years and to lean out as much as possible. Him and I both being in Manhattan, Kansas aka Wild City, Kanziss lets me know how serious he is simply because I have not seen him at all since he had made that statement and commitment. I'm excited to see him back on stage and to see his hard work and confidence even higher than before and what a win would do for him! After months and months have gone by, here we are at Manhattan's first ever bodybuilding competition that I am aware of at the City Park stage. The announcer announces the age class that my daw Jafay is competing in and we are all clapping loudly waiting for Jafay to step out on stage and that's when we see him…Clapping had stopped and this is just about everyone's first time seeing him in months since he had gone into deep hiding to focus on this competition and here Jafay is weighing at least 55 pounds on stage, skin and bones. He looks so sick especially knowing that the last time I've had seen him he was 175 pounds and to drop 120 pounds in description and obsession to be so lean he is on the verge of death and has lost so much body muscle and fat that he had to clip his trunks on him for them to stay up and looking like a starved Holocaust victim and that's when Jafay slowly walks across the stage and he…………………………..*

Chicago, Jewelry And Mechanic Store--- *So apparently I had decided to drive straight to Chicago by myself to a jewelry store that also specializes in the mechanic field of old school cars for my 1971 Chevy Caprice. To be honest, this place is uniquely genius for this 2 in 1 idea to bring in more money for this company. I'm excited to see my car after nearly a year of it being hauled off to Illinois from Kansas. I'm walking up the block to the jewelry store/car shop after parking my car at a lot that of course you have to pay to park because the city is expensive and money is spent almost anywhere and everywhere you go in such a large and busy city. As I'm stepping closer and closer to the shop, that's when I walk in and I see jewelry at the front counter and behind a bunch of older White guys in black leather jackets looking like a redneck biker gang. I stop at the front counter and a skinny redneck biker gang looking guy comes up to the counter and asks me if there's anything he could help me with. That's when I looked at him but then past him there was a gumball machine that my eyes wanted to continuously look at for some reason, but I looked back at the guy at the front counter and I said "Yuh. I'm here to get my black 1971 Chevy Caprice. It was hauled in from Kansas." That's when the guy looks at me and says "Oh OK. That's your car?! Such a classic! Everyone loves it. We are close to getting it done. It will probably be another 3 hours to be honest with you and then it's all yours. Until then take all of this change right here." That's when that guy pulled out the top rack of jewelry from the glass counter and poured a whole bunch of change all over it and he said "It's all yours!" I looked at this fool like "What the fuhh?!" But it was a lot of change and that's free money. This was probably about 30 pounds worth of change that I was going to take. The weird thing about it was that it was as if he wanted me to take that first row of jewelry too, but* *that sounded like a set up. As I'm grabbing handfuls of change and stuffing as much in my pockets that I could that's when I told him "I'm gonna step outside right quick to get some bags to fill them up with all the change that I could because this money can and will be used to pay for the repair of my car. As I walked halfway down the block, that's when I remembered I had my bag on my back that I could not only fill up with change, but the big ziploc bags I keep in my bag as well. So I turned around to go back into the shop and as I walked in I noticed how everyone in there was acting weird and that's when they looked at me and I put my ziploc bags in the air and I told them "I'm here to collect the rest of the change!" As I stepped to the glass counter I pointed at the skinny White guy that was at the counter with me earlier and I told him "Could you come here and help me with this?" I wanted him right there with me because with the jewelry underneath I didn't want to be accused of stealing any jewelry and I'm not even a fan of jewelry like that. He walks up to the glass counter and helps me put this change in the bag and I'm watching him carefully as he does so. After we had put the change in the bag which took us about 5 or so minutes that's when I said "Thank you! I'll be back in about 3 hours. I'm gonna go exploring the city for a little bit." That's when that skinny guy says "Have fun!" As he's putting the jewelry back into the glass case. I stepped out of the shop and took in a deep breath of fresh air as I stepped to my right and into more of Chicago's scenery. I'm walking block after block looking at the big buildings, the busy traffic, and everything else that I don't see on the regular in Kansas. After about 5 or 6 blocks that's when I ran into someone that I was not expecting to see at all out here that is from my hometown of Manhattan, Kansas. The chances of seeing a person out of nowhere like this from states away in such a big city such as Chicago unexpectedly is frazy to even think about. It's LaTitts. She's out here with an older Black guy in a suit which is frazy to me because LaTitts is a Black woman that has always been into White guys so this is definitely something new plus she has not really said much to me since high school so for her to be excited to see me and to say "Hi" is definitely out of the norm. We hugged one another and stepped back and then that's when I had tried to remember where the shop was and I………………………..*

Nipple Out--- *I am back at my favorite job I have ever worked at which is Ag Press. This time the staff is completely different, but the set up and the equipment in the building is the same as it was when I worked there. I'm in the office with Samuella being my manager which is frazy because she was the manager at the sportswear company I had worked at. She's talking to me about some shit that I can't really even focus on as she has a paper out reading something, but her titty has popped out over her red shirt and her nipple is big and juicy and ready to be sucked on and I can't help but to stare at it as I lowered my head down to put my eyes and mouth level with her nipple until she had pulled her shirt up to cover her titty as she continued to talk as if nothing was out of the room. I still wasn't paying attention to shit she was saying so I just asked "Can I suck your titty?" That's when she had looked at me and just busted out laughing and said "Uh no!" That's when I then said "I don't mean right now or at work." Then that's when she said "No!" So I stood up from the desk and chair and I went to the office door and left and walked past the machinery to the vending machines to look for a selection and that's when I noticed how some of the selections were barely in the ring so I rocked the vending machine and knocked a few snacks down, but the more and more that I rocked the machine the more and more that other snacks were loosening up. With that effect I kept rocking the vending machine* *to get more and more snacks to the bottom of the machine and the bottom was beginning to pile up and when I decided that I would get enough snacks that's when I started pulling my snacks out and when I could grab as many as I could that's when I had stood up to go to my machine and to put my snacks up, that was until I saw Samuella behind me with both of her titties out of her shirt this time and she says to me…………………………..*

<u>Young Spanish Fly In N.Y.---</u> *Here I am in the big and busy beautiful New York City! It's late night and I'm at the top floor of this beautiful hotel that I'm in the Royal Suites of. As I'm looking out of the big glass window thinking of the opportunities while being so high above the busy ground that's when I see this young Spanish feezy on the chair to my right laying on her side with her hand on her cheek with her elbow into the chair. I look over at her and she's smiling and she says with her thick accent "Did I scare you?" I said "A little bit. I woulda been more scared if you weren't so pretty." That's when she smiles and let's out this beautiful laugh. Then I heard light clicks of high heels come up from behind me and I see this tall slender blonde dub dub in a long, but skin tight black dress say to me "She likes you, but she doesn't know how to say it." That's when I jokingly say "I really have to learn to keep the lights on around here so I'm not hit with so many surprises. Is there anyone else in here that's gonna surprise me for a surprise birthday party for no one that has a birthday today? What do y'all think about New York? The big buildings and the pretty lights and the businesses. Does this fascinate you or is it just the everyday norm?" That's when the Spanish feezy was about to say something, but that blonde dub dub cuts her off by saying "She likes you, but she doesn't know how to tell you. She's 19 but wants you!" I looked back at the Spanish feezy and she looks good as fuhh and looks much more mature than a 19 year old. I'm thinking in my mind "There's a 13 year age difference, but she's still of age, but why isn't she telling me her age or how much she wants me? That's kinda weird to me." Then that's when the both of these women had…………………….*

<u>Suzy's Scrubs---</u> *I'm at this hospital on this hospital floor with this White feezy in front of me that's talking to me about a patient on the floor that she is working on and how the patient is in very bad health and acting out of control. She also goes on about how afraid she is to go back into the room and as she's talking and I'm looking at her scrubs that's when I noticed a big glob of white ink on the front of her shirt scrub or what appeared to look like white ink and that's when I pointed it out to her saying "Why is this white ink on your shirt? That looks like the type of ink that goes on screen printed shirts." As Suzy looks down to see what I was talking about that's when she looks at it for a couple of seconds and she slowly raises her hands to touch the spot and that's when she had slowly lifted her head back up to look at me and she let out this loud ass panicking scream with tears in her eyes and I'm so confused as to what the fuck is going on and what is actually on her shirt and that's when other nurses had rushed into the room that Suzy and I are in and that's when Suzy faints and falls right down to the ground and everyone rushes to her aid and that's when……………………..*

<u>On The SouthSide Again?---</u> *Here I am stepping up the sidewalk of my mom's duplex on the SouthSide of my hometown of Manhattan, Kansas aka Wild City, Kanziss. It's sunny outside and I'm going to the door as if I'm knocking on it to ask for my younger self to come outside because it's been years since my mom, my sisters, or I have lived here, but here I am like I'm* *back in time to talk to myself as if I am to give myself the best advice or a ride along for future preparation. As I get this strong nostalgic feeling walking up the small staircase to open the white screen door and to knock on the door and to ring the doorbell that's when I shut the screen door and turned around to wait for my mom, my sisters or my younger self to open the door. I looked at the white van that my mom used to just keep parked on the side street of the house that I'm driving now that has a bunch of K-State students in it dressed in purple with WildCats on the front of their shirts and most of them being dub dubs. I look at the van and them and they are all smiley and looking back at me waving as I waved back and that's when I could hear footsteps from inside the duplex come to the front door and the front door unlock and it pulling the white screen door in a little bit with the suction and pull and that's when I had turned around to see………………………..*

<u>About The Author</u>

Y'all haven't heard about him yet? The bodybuilding, inspirational, rapping, authentic book king booking author from Manhattan, Kansas aka Wild City, Kanziss named Bryan Vereen? The soon to be 32 year old that has written his 12th book that you now have your hands on and are about to read due to the curiosity of the cover and what a man of so many trades could have going through his mind? Yuh, Bryan Vereen with yet another book of dreams. Not only is he an advocate for living out YOUR dreams and writing down your goals, plans, and dreams, but to literally write down your dreams. The things that go through our mind that we wonder what made us think of that and why we are in rest and why certain dreams go to and through our head. How is it that we can have so many different dreams throughout our life as if they can never run out of creativity or a storyline? Don't you ever think about that? How come our dreams are all different throughout the years. Our minds don't replay the same dream over and over and the people we see in our minds that we wonder where or how they got into our subconscious mind. The reason for this book title is simple, WE all have dreams that most of them never end leaving that suspense. We wake up right before our dreams get to the really good part that makes you question what could have happened. That's what is so YOUnique to dreams in Bryan's opinion and that's why he writes them. Writing to look back and have the memory of the memos and the mental movies and entertainment we have while we are sleeping and not even watching the TV as our dreams could be more entertaining than our favorite movie or movies to be honest. Our minds and bodies are the movie directors and ourself being the actor/actresses as well. Isn't that a creative way to think about it? From what started off as dreams were all supposed to be songs, but with the constant dreams and the stories in Bryan Vereen's mind he figured why not turn his dreams into stories on paper. Why not? To love the mind and thinking and to somewhat understand and make more sense of it as we live on a daily basis is amazingly unique. To have no dreams one night to multiple dreams another makes you want to figure out what it is that causes dreams and specifically our dreams. With yet another creative and well put together book you will be entertained with not only what goes through Bryan Vereen's mind through his songs, but through his sleep and how we should make it a habit to memorize and do something special that comes to our mind just like we should with all of our great ideas when we are awake, aware, and conscious. Stay tuned for more books by this creative and YOUnique author and learn as you turn the pages as well. This father of 5 utilizes his time well and has so many business ventures in the works and on the way and he is honored to have you a part of it as this is just a small percentage of the things he has in mind (literally literal) that is on paper to be more physical and leave a bigger impact. The midwest is best the fool with the big chest. To never let any obstacle or challenge prevent you from being great even when times are rough and you have been against so many odds. Read UP! And write DOWN! YOUR thoughts and ideas and continue to support this man of many many great things that time and talent should be seen, heard, and used. Asiago!! NO fake EXcuse, face the truth, and taste the proof!! Face YOUR fears and taste the tears!

Like, Follow, or Subscribe to ME on my Social Media Platforms!!!!!

Follow me on SnapChat @nappyvereen

My clothing apparel "Versuhtyle Fitness and Motivation
https://teamstore.gtmsportswear.com/versuhtylefitness

Follow me on Instagram @NappyVereen

PayPal.me/nappyvereen

Venmo @NappyVereen

Cash App @ $NappyVereen

Like my fan page @http://www.facebook.com/nappyvereen7

Follow me on Twitter @Versuhtylefools or at @nappyvereen

Subscribe to my YouTube channel!

Follow me on Instagram @NappyVereen

PayPal.me/nappyvereen

Venmo @NappyVereen

Cash App @ $NappyVereen

Like my fan page @http://www.facebook.com/nappyvereen7

Follow me on Twitter @Versuhtylefools or at @nappyvereen

Subscribe to my YouTube channel!

https://fultonbooks.com/books/?book=keep-telling-yourself-that

https://omny.fm/shows/friday-night-author-roundtable/04-03-20-author-roundtable-142?in_playlist=friday-night-author-roundtable!podcast

VERSUNTYLE
FITNESS
THE DUMBBELL GUY

Versuhtyle Fitness & Motivation

I reFUSE
By Bryan
"Nappy"
Vereen
AkA
Topick!
Mental Movies

Dreams After
the Wake
By Bryan "Nappy"
Vereen
AkA Topick!

The Wake of Dreams
By Bryan "Nappy"
Vereen AkA Topick!

Quotes of Growth
By Bryan "Nappy" Vereen
Ak A Topick!
Abides

KEEP TELLING
Yourself THAT

And Then I Woke Up
By Bryan "Nappy" Vereen
AkA Topiat

versuhtyle fitness & motivation clothes
VERSUHTYLE FITN
Nutrition Facts
VERSUHTYLE FITNESS
Nutrition Facts
Get it now Asiago! @NappyVereen
LiveCollage

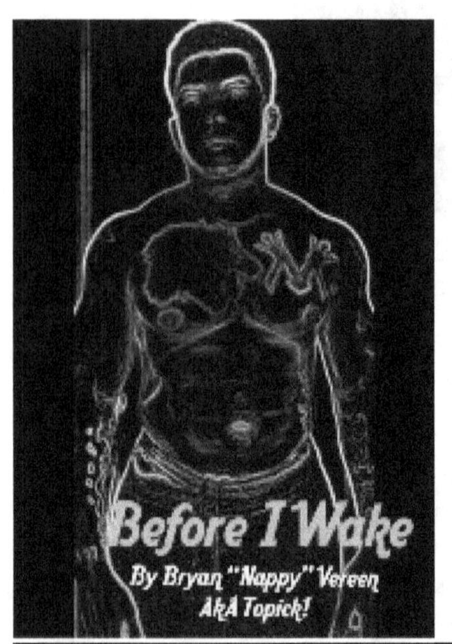

Before I Wake
By Bryan "Nappy" Vereen
AkA Topick!

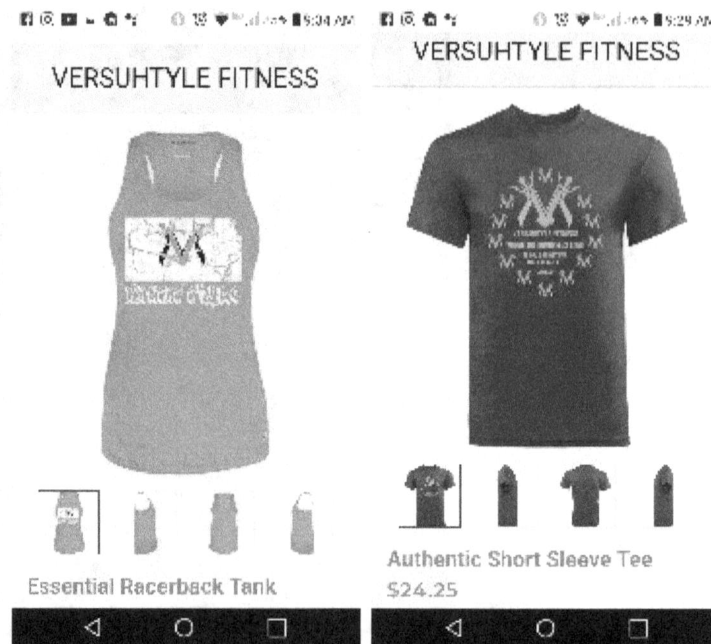

VERSUHTYLE FITNESS
Essential Racerback Tank
VERSUHTYLE FITNESS
Authentic Short Sleeve Tee
$24.25

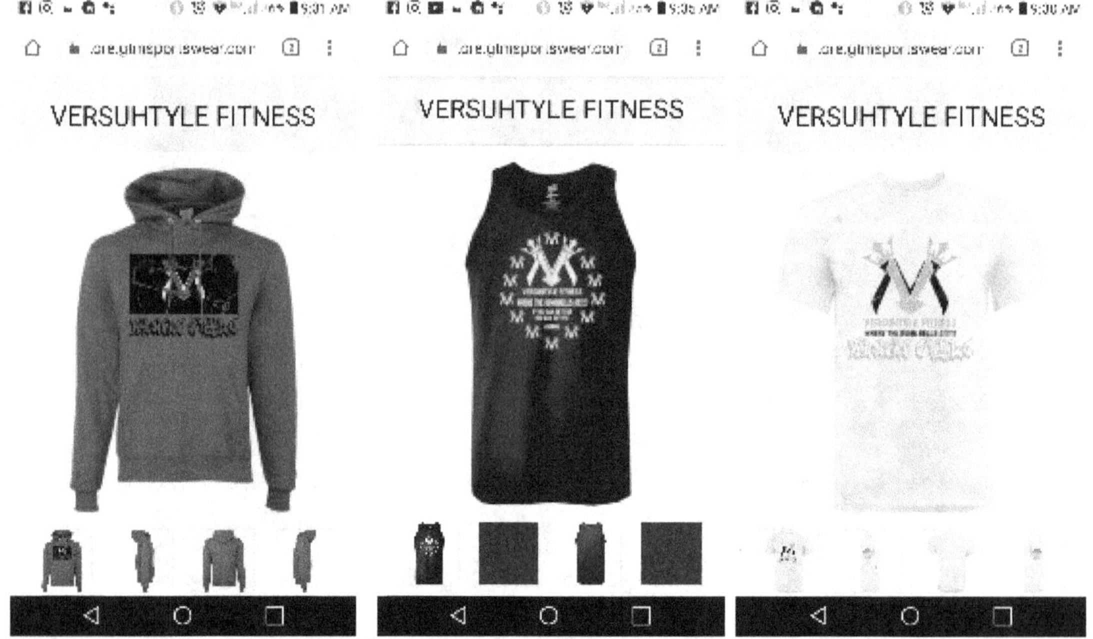

VERSUHTYLE FITNESS
VERSUHTYLE FITNESS
VERSUHTYLE FITNESS

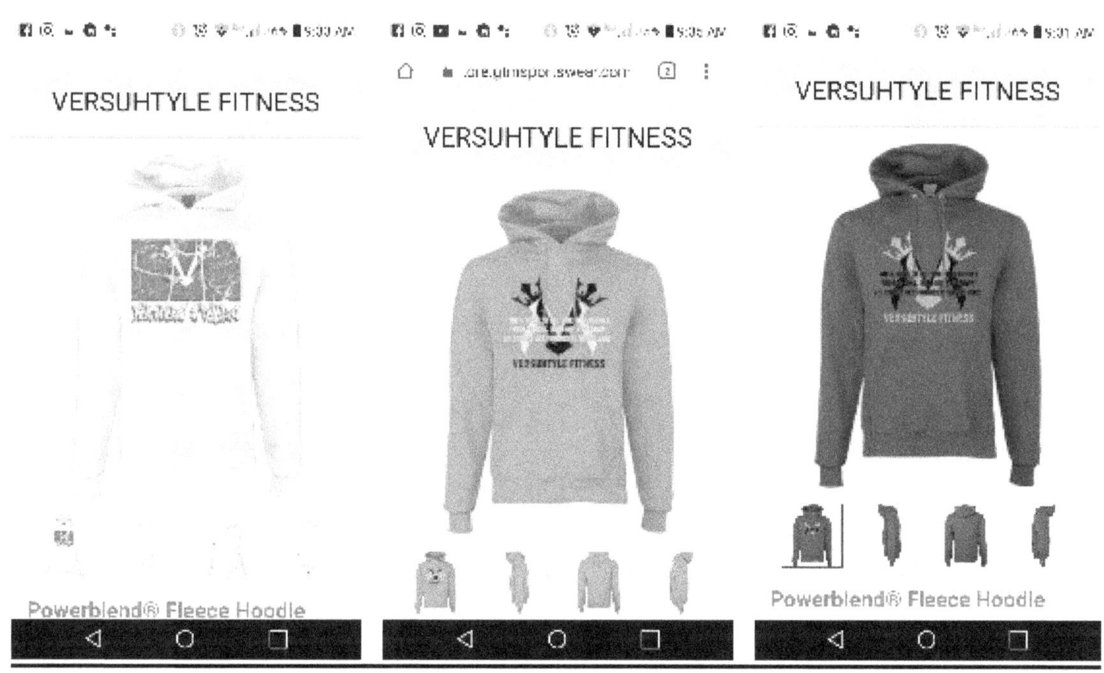
VERSUHTYLE FITNESS
VERSUHTYLE FITNESS
VERSUHTYLE FITNESS
Powerblend® Fleece Hoodle
Powerblend® Fleece Hoodle

VERSUHTYLE FITNESS
VERSUHTYLE FITNESS
Powerblend® Fleece Jogger